Passion Play

by Sarah Ruhl

A SAMUEL FRENCH ACTING EDITION

🎩 SAMUEL
FRENCH

FOUNDED 1830

NEW YORK HOLLYWOOD LONDON TORONTO

SAMUELFRENCH.COM

ISBN 978-0-573-69908-5   Printed in U.S.A.   #29778

MUSIC USE NOTE

Licensees are solely responsible for obtaining formal written permission from copyright owners to use copyrighted music in the performance of this play and are strongly cautioned to do so. If no such permission is obtained by the licensee, then the licensee must use only original music that the licensee owns and controls. Licensees are solely responsible and liable for all music clearances and shall indemnify the copyright owners of the play and their licensing agent, Samuel French, Inc., against any costs, expenses, losses and liabilities arising from the use of music by licensees.

IMPORTANT BILLING AND CREDIT REQUIREMENTS

All producers of *PASSION PLAY must* give credit to the Author of the Play in all programs distributed in connection with performances of the Play, and in all instances in which the title of the Play appears for the purposes of advertising, publicizing or otherwise exploiting the Play and/or a production. The name of the Author *must* appear on a separate line on which no other name appears, immediately following the title and *must* appear in size of type not less than fifty percent of the size of the title type.

In addition the following credit *must* be given in all programs and publicity information distributed in association with this piece:

**PASSION PLAY, PART 3 was originally commissioned by
Arena Stage, Washington, DC
(Molly Smith, Artistic Director; Stephen Richard, Executive Director)**

An early version of *PASSION PLAY* was produced in workshop at the Tristan Bates Theatre in London in July 2002. It was directed by Mark Wing-Davey; the design was by Madeline Herbert and the lighting design was by Emma Chapman. The cast was as follows:

PONTIUS. . . . . Colin Tierney/Tim Welton
JOHN. . . . . Oliver Chris/Oliver Dimsdale/Paul Ready
MARY 1 . . . . Kate Maravan
MARY 2 . . . . Annabel Capper
VISITNG FRIAR, ENGLISHMAN. . . . . Alan Cox
VILLAGE IDIOT . . . . Liz White/Nathalie Armin/Hayley Carmichael
CARPENTER 1. . . . . Peter Warnock/Michael Gilroy
CARPENTER 2. . . . . Patrick Brennan/Morgan James
DIRECTOR . . . . David Stevens
MACHINIST, GERMAN OFFICER . . . . Tim Welton/James Albrecht
QUEEN ELIZABETH, HITLER, REAGAN . . . . Scott Handy/Catherine Tate
SHEPHERD . . . . Danny Sapani/James Albrecht
SHEPHERDESS, BIRD. . . . . Louise Bolton
OLD LADY. . . . . Rita Davies

PASSION PLAY received its world premiere at Arena Stage (Molly Smith, Artistic Director; Edgar Dobie, Managing Director) in Washington, D.C., on September 2, 2005. It was directed by Molly Smith; the set design was by Scott Bradley, the costume design was by Linda Cho, the lighting design was by Joel Moritz, the sound design and original music were by Andre Pluess; the dramaturg was Mark Bly and the stage manager was Amber Dickerson. The cast was as follows:

PONTIUS, FOOT SOLDIER, P, ENSEMBLE . . . . Felix Solis
JOHN, ERIC, J, ENSEMBLE . . . . Howard W. Overshown
MARY 1, ENSEMBLE . . . . Kelly Brady
MARY 2, ENSEMBLE . . . . Carla Harting
VISITING FRIAR, VISITING ENGLISHMAN,
        VA 1, ENSEMBLE. . . . . Edward James Hyland
VILLAGE IDIOT, VIOLET, ENSEMBLE. . . . . Polly Noonan
CARPENTER 1, VA 2, ENSEMBLE. . . . . J. Fred Shiffman
CARPENTER 2, ENSEMBLE . . . . Lawrence Redmond
DIRECTOR, ENSEMBLE. . . . . Leo Erickson
MACHINIST, GERMAN OFFICER,
    YOUNG DIRECTOR, ENSEMBLE. . . . . Karl Miller
QUEEN E LI ZABETH, HITLER, REAGAN,
        NIXON, ENSEMBLE . . . . Robert Dorfman
ENSEMBLE . . . . Parker Dixon

PASSION PLAY was produced at the Goodman Theatre (Robert Falls, Artistic Director; Roche Schulfer, Executive Director) in Chicago on September 15, 2007. It was directed by Mark Wing-Davey; the set design was by Allen Moyer, the costume design was by Gabriel Berry, the lighting design was by James F. Ingalls, the sound design was by Cecil Averett, the projection design was by Ruppert Bohle; the dramaturg was Tanya Palmer, the production stage manager was Joseph Drummond and the stage manager was T. Paul Lynch. The cast was as follows:

PONTIUS THE FISH GUTTER, FOOT SOLDIER, P ...... Brian Sgambati
JOHN THE F ISHERMAN, ERIC, J .... Joaquin Torres
MARY 1 .... Kristen Bush
MARY 2 .... Nicole Wiesner
VISITING FRIAR, VISITING ENGLISHMAN,
    YOUNG DIRECTOR .... Alan Cox
VILLAGE IDIOT, VIOLET .... Polly Noonan
CARPENTER 1, TOWNSMAN .... Brendan Averett
CARPENTER 2, TOWNSMAN .... Keith Kupferer
DIRECTOR .... Craig Spidle
MACHINIST, GERMAN OFFICER, VA .... John Hoogenakker
QUEEN ELIZABETH, HITLER, REAGAN .... T. Ryder Smith
ENSEMBLE .... Tiffany Bedwell, Jeremy Clark,
                              Kyle Lemieux, Ron Rains, Jayce Ryan

PASSION PLAY was produced at Yale Repertory Theatre (James Bundy, Artistic Director; Victoria Nolan, Managing Director) in New Haven, CT, on September 19, 2008. It was directed by Mark Wing-Davey; the set design was by Allen Moyer, the costume design was by Ilona Somogyi, the lighting design was by Stephen Strawbridge, the sound design was by Charles Coes; the production dramaturg was Colin Mannex and the stage manager was James Mountcastle. The cast was as follows:

PONTIUS THE FISH GUTTER .... Felix Solis
JOHN THE FISHERMAN .... Joaquin Torres
MARY 1 .... Susan Pourfar
MARY 2 .... Nicole Wiesner
VISITING FRIAR, VISITING ENGLISHMAN, VA .... Thomas Jay Ryan
VILLAGE IDIOT, VIOLET .... Polly Noonan
CARPENTER 1 .... Brendan Averett
CARPENTER 2 .... Austin Durant
DIRECTOR .... Keith Reddin
MACHINIST, GERMAN OFFICER,
    YOUNG DIRECTOR .... Dieterich Gray
QUEEN ELIZABETH, HITLER, REAGAN .... Kathleen Chalfant
ENSEMBLE .... Laura Esposito, Brian Hastert,
                   Slate Holmgren, Barret O'Brien, Luke Robertson

PASSION PLAY was produced by Epic Theatre Ensemble (Zak Berkman, Melissa Friedman, Ron Russell; Executive Directors) at The Irondale Center in Brooklyn, NY, on May 12, 2010. It was directed by Mark Wing-Davey; the set design was by Warren Karp and Allen Moyer, the costume design was by Gabriel Berry and Antonia Ford-Roberts, the lighting design was by David Weiner, additional music was composed by David Van Tieghem; the associate director was Scott Illingworth, the movement director was James Calder; the fight director was David Anzuelo, the dialect coach was Deborah Hecht and the stage manager was Iris O'Brien. The cast was as follows:

PONTIUS THE FISH GUTTER . . . . Dominic Fumusa

JOHN THE FISHERMAN . . . . Hale Appleman

MARY 1 . . . . Kate Turnbull

MARY 2 . . . . Nicole Wiesner

VISITING FRIAR, VISITING ENGLISHMAN . . . . Daniel Pearce

VILLAGE IDIOT, VIOLET . . . . Polly Noonan

CARPENTER 1 . . . . Brendan Averett

CARPENTER 2 . . . . Godfrey L. Simmons, Jr.

DIRECTOR . . . . Keith Reddin

MACHINIST, GERMAN OFFICER,
   YOUNG DIRECTOR . . . . Alex Podulke

QUEEN ELIZABETH, HITLER, REAGAN . . . . T. Ryder Smith

AUTHOR'S NOTES

I started writing this play fourteen years ago after rereading a childhood book which includes an account of Oberammergau in the early 1900s. In this old fashioned narrative, the man who played Christ was actually so holy as to have become a living embodiment. The woman who played Mary was, in real life, just as pure as the Virgin. I started thinking, how would it shape or misshape a life to play a biblical role year after year? How are we scripted? Where is the line between authentic identity and performance? And is there, in fact, such a line?

The first act is set in 1575 in England, when Queen Elizabeth was about to shut down the Passion Plays in order to control religious representation. Not many towns still performed the Passion in 1575; the village of Act One is, then, itself something of an anachronism, oddly suspended between the middle ages and the Renaissance. In 1575, Queen Elizabeth banned religious plays altogether; up until then, over one hundred towns in the British Isles performed the Passion. Meanwhile, Elizabeth, who was excommunicated by the Pope in 1571, increased measures in the 1570s to cleanse England of Papal trappings, including Jesuits. Ordinary Catholics often housed priests in what they called "priest-holes" in order to maintain Catholic rites.

The second act moves to Oberammergau, Germany – a town where the Passion Play, begun in the Middle Ages, even now continues to be played every ten years. Many narratives describe Oberammergau as a living picture of the New Testament, ignoring the fact that, in 1934, the director of the Passion was already a member of the Nazi party. The actor who played Christ and the actress who played the Virgin Mary were also early party members. By 1947, every actor in the play had at one time been a Nazi, with the exception of the men who played, ironically, Judas and Pontius Pilate. (The play takes liberties with these historical facts.) As late as 1946, the village of Oberammergau denied knowing anything about concentration camps, although Dachau (where Oberammergau's one Jew was sent during the war) was only seventy-five miles away.

The Passion Play, which often incited pogroms during Easter when performed in medieval Germany, became a historical perversion during the war, seen with our contemporary lens. In 1934, Hitler saw the Passion and was greeted with open arms. He came a second time on August 13, 1934 – six weeks after "Night of the Long Knives," when Hitler purged his leadership of known homosexuals, Communists, and Jews. Act Two of Passion Play quotes the 19th century Oberammergau script (famous for its anti-Semitism), as well as quoting a speech Hitler made at a dinner, expressing his admiration for the Oberammergau Passion in 1942. Everything else in the play is an invention. I am indebted to Saul Friedman and James Shapiro for their careful research.

It should be said that, since the war, Oberammergau has made many attempts to reform their Passion Play; has invited Jewish scholars and has revised their text in order to reflect a more ecumenical view. Many Passion Plays have enlisted the Anti-Defamation league to get it right, or at least, more right. And yet, even today, we are plunged into the same kind of moral/aesthetic debates, as when Mel Gibson took up the mantle of the Passion, which had one of the biggest viewerships, ironically, in the Arab world. But more people talked about "Passion-dollars" – the surprise commercial success of the movie – than they did about the dangers of focusing the Gospel story on violent scape-goating.

Years after beginning Parts One and Two of *Passion Play* (which I began with the encouragement of Paula Vogel) I returned to the cycle. I discovered that there was a Passion Play in Spearfish, South Dakota, started by an actor from Germany in the 1940s. I felt that I had to continue the story. Serendipitously, Arena Stage in Washington D.C. asked me to write a play about America, and I figured that there's nothing more American than the nexus of religion, politics, and the theatre. Especially when it seemed as if we were in the midst of an unacknowledged holy war, conducted by a man who felt himself to be appointed by God (he must have been appointed by someone, he wasn't appointed by the popular vote in 2000). Never had the medieval world and the digital age seemed so oddly conjoined. I found myself fascinated by how leaders use, misuse and legislate religion for their own political aims, and how leaders turn themselves into theatrical icons. Queen Elizabeth, wearing layers and layers of make-up, "married" herself to England; Hitler took photographs of himself gesticulating until he got it right; Ronald Reagan had miraculous and natural powers as an actor. But what is the difference between acting as performance and acting as moral action? It is no accident that we refer to theaters of war.

More and more, it seems to me that the separation between church and state is coming into question in our country. We are a divided nation. And the more divided we are, the less we talk about what divides us. The left is perceived of as anti-religious ideological secularists; the right as religious zealots. But whatever happened to the founding father's rationale for separating church and state? More devotion was possible, and more kinds of devotion would be possible, the less the state controlled religious rhetoric. More devotion, and more conversation about devotion, would be possible with that freedom. I miss that conversation, and I think theater is a good place for it. To my mind, devotion is like a quality of light – how is it possible to legislate the quality of light? It would be like legislating the invisible moments that happen in a theater. And ultimately, this play is about those moments – about how actors wring moments out of their private lives in order bear witness in the community.

Ideally, *Passion Play* (Parts One, Two, and Three) would be performed all together in one evening (it should run about three hours plus intermissions) or else in rotating repertory. Together, the three parts form a cycle play – alone, they do something different, but they can technically stand alone. If in repertory, I suggest doing Parts One and Two on one night, and Part Three on the next. If the resources of one theater are too limited to produce the entire cycle, I can imagine two theaters in one city collaborating to put the cycle up together. In the original guild productions of the Passion, the carpenters in the village would handle the crucifixion scene and the bakers would handle the Last Supper. Perhaps our theatrical communities could borrow from the primitive guild model.

I wrote the first draft of *Passion Play*, Part Three before the 2004 election, with a great sense of urgency. It's easy to feel powerless as the great political wheels turn, financed by enormous wealth. But then you get to thinking about what starts every grass-roots revolution – people organizing in one room. Luckily that very special right is protected by our Constitution. And as ill-suited as some theater artists are to some meanings of the word "organization," there is one thing all of us tend to do well, and that is to organize people to come to one room. It is not that the play you are about to read is a political treatise – not at all – but it does provide us with another occasion to be in one room together as we continue to meditate on the relationship of community to political icons. And to meditate on what we can do to affect change in very solemn times indeed.

– Sarah Ruhl

CHARACTER BREAKDOWN FOR ENTIRE CYCLE

The full play requires eleven actors. Each actor retains a semblance of his or her role when the play jumps in time and space. For example, Pontius the Fish Gutter becomes a Foot Soldier in Part Two, and a Vietnam vet named "P" in Part Three. There is some flexibility in how the Carpenters and Machinist are reincarnated in Part Three. The play is an ensemble piece, and all the players help to create the world of the play within the play.

Part One *England, 1575*	*Part Two* *Germany, 1934*	*Part Three* *South Dakota, 1969—the present*
PONTIUS THE FISH GUTTER (plays Pontius Pilate and Satan)	**FOOTSOLDIER** (plays Pontius Pilate)	**P** (plays Ponitus Pilate and Satan)
JOHN THE FISHERMAN (plays Jesus and Adam)	**ERIC** (plays Jesus)	**J** (plays Jesus)
MARY 1 (plays the Virgin Mary and Eve)	**ELSA** (plays the Virgin Mary)	**MARY 1** (plays the Virgin Mary)
MARY 2 (plays Mary Magdalen)	**MARY 2** (plays Mary Magdalen)	**MARY 2** (plays Mary Magdalen)
VISITING FRIAR	**VISITING ENGLISHMAN, OR SIMON LILLY**	**VA PSYCHIATRIST**
VILLIAGE IDIOT	**VIOLET**	**VIOLET**
CARPENTER 1, SAM (plays the angel Gabriel)	**CARPENTER 1, JOHANN**	**CARPENTER1/ENSEMBLE**
CARPENTER 2, SIMON (plays Joseph)	**CARPENTER 2/ LUDWIG**	**CARPENTER 2/ ENSEMBLE**
DIRECTOR	**DIRECTOR, ROCHUS SCHALLHAMMER**	**DIRECTOR**
MACHINIST (plays an emperor)	**GERMAN OFFICER**	**YOUNG DIRECTOR**
QUEEN ELIZABETH	**HITLER**	**PRESIDENT REAGAN, QUEEN ELIZABETH, HITLER**

This play is for Paula Vogel.

PASSION PLAY

PART ONE

A village in Northern England, Spring, 1575

CHARACTERS

PONTIUS THE FISH GUTTER. . . . . plays Pontius and Satan
JOHN THE FISHERMAN . . . . plays Jesus and Adam
MARY 1 . . . . plays the Virgin Mary and Eve
MARY 2 . . . . plays Mary Magdalen
VISITING FRIAR
VILLAGE IDIOT
CARPENTER 1 or **SAM** . . . . plays the angel Gabriel
CARPENTER 2 or **SIMON** . . . . plays Joseph
DIRECTOR
MACHINIST . . . . plays an emperor
QUEEN ELIZABETH. preferably a man in drag

SET

The suggestion of the sea.
A playing space.

PROLOGUE

CHORUS.

We make our play in England.
In the North
By the sea
In the open air of England.
The Virgin Queen is on her throne
The Catholics are mostly done.
Take pity on our simple play –
we've no fancy lights
only the bare light of day.
The good Lord tells us,
to be most simple is to be most good –
so here is honest rough-hewn wood.
We ask you, dear audience to use your eyes, ears, your
most inward sight
for here is day *(a painted sun)*
and here is night *(a painted moon).*
And now, the play.

SCENE 1: BUILDING THE ROOD

A man on a cross. The sound of sawing.
At first we are not sure whether or not this is a real
crucifixion.
Carpenter 1 (Sam) measures John the Fisherman from
head to toe.

CARPENTER 1. You have g–grown.

JOHN. I'm afraid so. I wish my bones would not make such
work for you year after year.

CARPENTER 1. You cannot stop your bones from gr-gr–
growing.

JOHN. My cousin's bones stopped growing three years ago,
and his bones have troubled no seamstress with new
stitches since. Perhaps he should play my part.

CARPENTER 2. Oh, but he's a limp wee little thing. Gutted
his hand when he meant to gut a flounder. And now
his back's as crooked as the road to hell!

JOHN. Now you mustn't make fun of poor Pontius.

CARPENTER 1. What mmmm mighty arms you have! You
could swing many a fi-fi-fine lady on those br-brawny
arms.

JOHN. You could knock me down easily, Sam!

CARPENTER 1. Nnno. I would never h-h-hurt my John boy.

CARPENTER 2. Now me and him may be twins, but we're
as different as two peas in different pods. He likes his
ale light, I like it dark. He likes Sundays, I detest 'em.
I like blondes, and he likes his brunettes, don't you
there, Sam?

The Sky Turns Red.

JOHN. Why there's that red light again!

CARPENTER 2. So it is! What the devil…

CARPENTER 1. It's been a' creeping and a cr-cr-crawling
into the cracks in the windows! It makes me afffraid.

They stand, transfixed. The light disperses and becomes natural.

CARPENTER 2. Oh well, I suppose the sun must be angry about something. Only one more little nail.

He pounds in a nail.

There. Your measurements, my good man, have been taken.

He helps John off the cross.
Exit Carpenter 1 and John.
Simon stays behind to tell the audience:

I have blisters and splinters and all for the glory of God. My father's father was a carpenter. My father's father's father was a carpenter. We all have blisters and splinters in our fingers and all for the glory of God.

SCENE 2: PONTIUS AND A TRAVELING FRIAR

Pontius, to the audience:

PONTIUS. All my life I've wanted to play Christ...if only, I thought, they put me on a cross, I would feel holy, I would walk upright. And every year my cousin plays the Savior.

I want to kill my cousin. No – I want – when he is on the cross – and if I left him on just the slightest bit too long – and if the pretend nails were real...then they would nail me to the cross, and I would follow him to glory.

My cousin is a good man – ah, the tingling in my head again – something pulling – like a string at the top – a puppet – up down up down, string.

Today the sky turned red, the sky turned red, and we should kneel down and take notice but everyone's too busy eating their bloody porridge!

On the other side of the stage, a Visiting Friar appears.
He is in disguise.

VISITING FRIAR. *(addressing the audience)* Today I walked far and far until I noticed that the shrubbery had changed and I was out of my province. And then – the sky turned red! At two in the afternoon! If shivers didn't crawl up and down my spine like worms...

PONTIUS. *(to the audience)* My cousin is nothing but a bastard!

VISITING FRIAR. *(to the audience)* I will conceal myself behind a tree and observe this young man.

PONTIUS. *(to the audience)* He is a thorn in my side that must be plucked out. If I were a woman I could bake this malice into my bread, but as it is, I am a man and I must make this malice a knife. I will store my acorns of malice, I will guard them and I will harvest them in the spring.

Pontius notices the Visiting Friar and changes his face.

PONTIUS. Hello, traveler! What brings you to our little town? New faces are seldom seen here.

VISITING FRIAR. I come from a neighboring village but am tired and require water. Are you not the famed village that plays the Passion, scattering tales of its holiness across the land?

PONTIUS. We are that very village, sir.

VISITING FRIAR. Not many towns dare in these dark days to play the Passion in England.

PONTIUS. Aye. This town is slow to change.

VISITING FRIAR. Are you then the same town famed for a most beautiful and graceful young man who plays the part of Christ?

PONTIUS. He is, in point of fact – my cousin.

VISITING FRIAR. Your family must be proud of such a relation.

PONTIUS. My family is very proud of my cousin, I'm sure.

A grimace to the audience. A smile to the Visiting Friar.

VISITING FRIAR. And you? What do you play?

PONTIUS. Pontius Pilate – and Satan.

VISITING FRIAR. Ah! To be sure!

Pontius grimaces to the audience. A smile to the Friar.

PONTIUS. Would you like to take a drink of water at my home?

VISITING FRIAR. I would be most grateful. Perhaps I can meet the famed cousin of yours.

PONTIUS. By all means!
(to the audience) Between gritted teeth, between bloody gritted teeth!

SCENE 3: JOHN THE FISHERMAN'S KITCHEN, DAY

VISITING FRIAR. You're just as comely and upright as they say.

JOHN. Thank you.

VISITING FRIAR. With the same dimple in the chin.

JOHN. You must be hungry. Can I make you some eggs, sir?

VISITING FRIAR. I would be honored to eat an egg made by your holy hands.

(checking the door, in low tones) Young man, can I trust you're a Catholic?

JOHN. We are all Catholic in our private hearts though we have no public house of worship left. The stage is our house of worship.

The Visiting Friar takes off his disguise, revealing a priest's cowl.

John kneels down and kisses the hand of the Friar.

God save you! Is it not dangerous for you to stay here? Are they not catching priests and putting them into prison?

VISITING FRIAR. Aye. We're hidden in closets and priest-holes all over England.

JOHN. And are you now in need of a hiding place?

VISITING FRIAR. Aye. But I would not dream of putting you in danger.

JOHN. Stay with us.

VISITING FRIAR. I know now why they tell tales of your Christ. You have His spirit.

JOHN. You really mustn't believe such things, good Friar. Perhaps you'd like to come to our rehearsal today. You could see the scaffolds that lift men up, the machinery that brings men down. You'll see that I'm no better than the tattered costume that I wear.

VISITING FRIAR. I would be honored to see the famed village rehearse.

SCENE 4: THE VILLAGE IDIOT

Day. The heavenly choir rehearses.
The Director conducts, and arranges their halos. The
Visiting Friar watches.
The Village Idiot sits cross-legged in the town square,
playing with a jack-in-the-box.
The sound of a musical jack-in-the-box crank.

THE VILLAGE IDIOT. In a time, in a time, in a time without...words – oh – pop – pop goes the weasel! *(laughs)* You have a strange ugly face, surprising to pop out at me! Why do you pop out at me? Do you like me, scary big nose? *(laughs again)*

DIRECTOR. Shut your mouth, village idiot!

VILLAGE IDIOT. *(to the jack-in-the-box)* Well, Jack, Big Director Man told us to shut our mouths – I shut your mouth. *(Stuffs him back in box.)* Now I want you out again to play with. *(Winding)* Bird of a heart, heart of a giant, big beast in the mouth of hell! Pop! Jack! You again – darling Jack, I thought I'd never see you again, shut down in that dark, dark box, your body all bent and twisted. *(Kisses him)* I'm sorry I put you in your box, dear Jack...

DIRECTOR. *(overlapping slightly)* I said, shut your mouth, village idiot! The heavenly choir rehearses!

VILLAGE IDIOT. The heavenly choir rehearses, oh, oh, the heavenly choir rehearses...no part for Jack or me, oh no. You just pop out of a box, don't you Jack? And I just wind you because things need to be wound – clocks – tick tick – hearts – tick tick – oh! Beautiful, beautiful Jack with your heart in a box.

The Director marches over and ties the Village Idiot to a stump, putting the Jack-in-the-Box a distance away.

Ahhhh! JACK! SAVE ME! It is dark and I am in the box...I'll close my eyes and make the sky turn red.... now...now....

The sky turns red.
The heavenly choir stops singing.
The heavenly choir looks up.

THE VILLAGE IDIOT. See that, Jack! Did you see?

SCENE 5: MARY AND MARY

*The Director and the half-naked figure of John the
Fisherman practice the crucifixion scene.*
The Visiting Friar looks on in disguise.
*Mary 1 and Mary 2 sit on the other side of the stage
under a tree.*
Mary 1 wears a halo.

MARY 2. Mary Magdalen was a whore because she pretended and that's like me – I'm a whore because I pretend things.

MARY 1. How do you know Mary Magdalen pretended things?

MARY 2. I don't know. I just know.

MARY 1. Oh, his acting is divine! Oh! Oh! His loincloth is slipping!

MARY 2. It is easy and fun to seduce men – you can pretend things, and it's fun to pretend – but then you have to bed them, and that is the boring part – you can hardly pretend anything interesting with your legs apart.

MARY 1. Boring! Why, Mary, your brain is addled. Milking cows is boring. Needlework is boring.

MARY 2. It's all one! At least with needlework, *I* work the needle and stitch where I please instead of lying like a tapestry only to be pricked. At least with cow-milking *I* squeeze the teet instead of standing swollen and mooing.

MARY 1. No, no, Mary. You can't possibly think milking cows and needlework and men-bedding are all one. Perhaps you've not found the right man.

MARY 2. Perhaps.

MARY 1. John, the Fisherman, for instance, he's handsome and true. And seeing him so oft in his rehearsal loincloth – it makes me pound and pound.

MARY 2. I've known John the Fisherman too long to fancy
him in a loincloth. I like to stick to my books. There's
a heap more amusement in one book than in a score
of beddings all alike.

MARY 1. And his muscles like a lion's, and golden too!

MARY 2. Hmmph.

*Mary 1 freezes, ogling John the Fisherman. Mary 2 turns
to the audience.*

When I was a child I noticed one day that all the girls
turned into strange flapping birds when the boys
walked by. Their eyes got huge and acquired wings, as
though cursed, wings for eyelashes to flutter and flap. I
thought the wings on their eyes might fly them to a different land altogether. I didn't turn into a bird around
anyone – I stayed quiet and very still.

MARY 1. Oh! Oh! His loincloth is slipping!

MARY 2. It's sinful to covet your own son, Mary. It's a sin, a
sin against God.

MARY 1. I didn't ask to play his mother.

MARY 2. I'm sure it's not right, Mary.

Perhaps we should switch roles.

I think my part has more scenes with John the Fisherman.

MARY 1. Oh!

MARY 2. Run find the director and ask! Go on!

Mary 1 runs off.

(looking after Mary 1) Yes, much better to play the Virgin
Mary – to have a baby – yes – I do like babies – and a
husband – yes, I do like men – I do – but not to bed the
one to get the other! No wonder she smiled so tenderly
in all the paintings. The happiest and best of women.

Enter the Director and Mary 1.

DIRECTOR. I'm sorry, ladies, but you've signed your contracts. And besides, *you* look like a saint *(to Mary 1)* and *you* look like a whore. *(points to Mary 2)* There's no getting around it. *(to Mary 2)* Look at that beauty mark and that gap between the teeth. And you've got a bit of a deformity in the chin – it just wouldn't do for the Virgin Mary to have a bit of deformity in the chin. *(to Mary 1)* And her smile. A smile like that would melt the devil's heart. But not mine. Now finish memorizing your parts, ladies. There's no time for all of this driveling anarchy.

Enter The Visiting Friar, in disguise.

VISITING FRIAR. Would anyone here like to confess their sins?

MARY 2. I would.

VISITING FRIAR. Meet me around the corner after dark.

SCENE 6: AT THE CONFESSIONAL

MARY 2. Forgive me Father, for I have sinned. I have dreams of women embracing me and kissing me full on the lips.

VISITING FRIAR. That is indeed a sin.

I want you to say twenty Hail Marys, thirty-two Our Fathers, and hang a crucifix above your bed.

MARY 2. But there is a crucifix above my bed, Father. And I find that I rather enjoy the dreams, though I try not to have them.

VISITING FRIAR. Now you mustn't enjoy such dreams, Mary. It addles a young girl's brain to play the role of a whore from a young age. I want you to say your penances, Mary, chew on a ginger root, and change parts with the shepherdess.

MARY 2. Oh, but she's not half so good as me, Father. I'll be good, so good! I'm good at pretending!

VISITING FRIAR. Now, Mary, I am looking after the salvation of your soul.

MARY 2. Yes, Father. *(pause)* Father, why is it wrong to dream of women kissing you full on the lips?

VISITING FRIAR. Ask God, Mary. Only God can explain, only God – the Father.

The Sky Turns Red.

MARY 2. Oh the sky, the sky, again the sky!

SCENE 7

Pontius sits on a stoop, cleaning his shoes with a knife.

PONTIUS. Last night the moon threw its head back, laughing at me – a white wedge – a laughing pitchfork – and tonight the moon sank down on his haunches – his face turned full at me – he looked bewildered and afraid. Had the fat white face of a dunce. You think I'm a bloody fool to speak of the moon, but who else will be a witness to my grief?

The doctor who birthed me, see, he didn't sew up my belly properly. Most people have got some skin between their guts and the air of the world, not me, not me. You can stick your finger way into my belly button, and when you pull it out it smells like gangrene, like fish.

I gut the fish. My cousin – he catches 'em. He don't have to see their innards. He don't have to talk to dead fish all day. He can talk to the sea. Me – I close my nose and I smell the stench of dead fish. I close my eyes and see dead fish coming at me in a parade.

He closes his eyes and huge beautiful fish puppets walk towards him as if in a parade. They surround him and undress him. They leave to the beating of drums. He turns to the audience. He blinks. The sound of the sea gurgles.

SCENE 8: NIGHT

Mary 1 kneels by her bed.

MARY 1. Hail Mary, full of grace...

(to the audience) I hate to sleep alone. My feet get cold.
I put socks on and then my feet get hot so I take them
off under the blankets but then my feet get cold again
in the night.

(putting her socks on) It's unnatural, cold and unnatural, this solitary sleeping. The sheep sleep together, all
woolly and warm. I get too lonesome to sleep alone. I
slept with my parents 'til I got too old. One time they
locked me out – I could hear why – strange sounds
coming from the bed. When I got old enough I found
men to sleep with – men with hair on their legs and
bellies to keep me warm at night. I go out walking
sometimes to find them.

She climbs down a rope and out of her window.

I've never been with child. Don't know why. Better not
to ask God.

John the Fisherman out walking in a shaft of light.

JOHN. Sometimes – tonight – a feeling of grace comes and
I feel peaceful and easy and ready to die but still aware
of the moon's beauty, like silver fish scales shedding.
Skin covers the world – luminous moonskin – and I
must step softly and slowly on it – the cobbled streets
have fish-skin, the trees have human skin – and it is
not fearsome, only slow and lovely and soft, but I must
be careful not to prick you and make you bleed.

Mary 1 walks toward him, carrying a jar.

MARY 1. Good evening.

JOHN. Good evening, Mary. What brings you into the night
air by yourself?

MARY 1. Uuum...My mother – she's sick – doctor told me
to trap the night air in a jar and bring it back to her.

JOHN. May I help?

Mary looks down, embarrassed.

MARY 1. Umm –

JOHN. I'd do anything to help you and your good mother, Mary.

MARY 1. Could you climb up that wagon, John, and trap that particular spot of air?

She hands him a jar and he climbs an abstracted wagon.

JOHN. This spot?

She scrutinizes him from behind.

MARY 1. Perhaps a little to the left.
And to the right. And up. Yes, that bit there.

JOHN. *(handing her the jar)* I hope this will do, Mary.

She smiles at him.

JOHN. Your mother…is she very sick?

MARY 1. My mother?….Oh yes…her belly….she swallowed something…

JOHN. I'm sorry, Mary. You know I would drink your sorrow if I could.

John escorts Mary 1 offstage.
Pontius appears from behind a bush.

PONTIUS. Always, always, always him!
I can cry
only out of one eye.
Only the left
and the right stays dry.
Dry as a bone
dry as a cunt
who's left alone.
Oh, God let me cry!
Out of both eyes, please God,
please God let me cry!

Same scene. Night.

Mary 1 climbs back into her bedroom window.

MARY 1. It will be a cold bed for me again tonight. He's chaste as a clam.

SCENE 9: THE FALL OF MAN – A REHEARSAL

Mary 1, the Director, Pontius and an apple.

DIRECTOR. In this scene, Mary, you are tempted by a delicious, ripe fruit. Your mouth should water. Now. Go.

PONTIUS. *(as Satan)* Eve! Eve!

MARY 1. *(as Eve)* Who is there?

SATAN/PONTIUS. I, a friend.
    And for thy good is the coming.
    Bite on boldly, be not abashed.

DIRECTOR. Don't be afraid, Pontius. Slink your skinny arm around her waist. There, there. Dangle the apple in front of her lips.

MARY 1. Then will I to thy teaching trust,
    And fang this fruit unto our food.

    She bites timidly into the apple.

DIRECTOR. Bite harder! The juice must dribble down your chin! Again!

MARY 1. Then will I to thy teaching trust,
    And fang this fruit unto our food.

    She bites the apple, hard, a large section of apple in her mouth.

PONTIUS. Oh!

DIRECTOR. Good.

SCENE 10: NIGHT

Pontius sits on a wagon, looking at stars.

PONTIUS. *(to the audience)* I gutted a fish today – I thought
it was dead – I slit open its belly – and five live fishes
squirmed out. They stunk of death. They wriggled and
wraggled in the guts of their mother and they died
one by one. The last one to go was a real wriggler. He
watched everyone go before him – he swam around in
their fishy guts – and then I slammed the knife down
on his back. I couldn't stand to see one so alone and
so alive, so I killed the poor devil to put it out of its
misery.

He sees Mary 1 offstage.

Hush – Mary walks. The smell of the moon follows
her. And her eyes follow my cousin. Would she kiss a
poor fishmonger? Would she wrap her arms around
the stench?

Mary 1 appears, holding a jar.

Miss Mary, why are you out walking at this time of
night?

MARY 1. You startled me.

PONTIUS. I didn't mean to frighten you, Mary.

MARY 1. There is little light from the moon tonight. The
trees cast their shadows on your face.

PONTIUS. I can see you. I can see you because I have stud-
ied your face in the dark of my bed before sleeping.

MARY 1. I am a Christian woman.

PONTIUS. Why are you out walking tonight?

He comes closer to her.

MARY 1. You smell of fish.

PONTIUS. I slit open their bellies all day. Why are you out
walking tonight?

MARY 1. I could sell you some rosewater. You could sprinkle
it over your hands.

PONTIUS. Oh, would you, Miss Mary?

MARY 1. Well…yes. Good night.

She turns to go.

PONTIUS. Don't go.
    (to the audience) She is a deer wrapped in brown velvet.
    She is the air breathing inside the body of a violin.
    (to her) Don't go.

MARY 1. It's late.

PONTIUS. According to who? The sun? The moon? It's
    early for the sun – he hasn't even woken from his nap.
    And it's only mid-afternoon for the moon, she's just
    barely risen. And you out walking…Owls don't fly out
    of their dens for no reason.

MARY 1. You play tricks with words.

PONTIUS. Do you play tricks, Mary?

MARY 1. Certainly not.

*They look at each other. He seizes her. They kiss. She
drops the jar.*

The night air. You've spilled it.

*Pontius gets on the wagon
and traps the same bit of air that John trapped.
He gives it to her.
She pities him. Kisses him.*

You don't taste like other men.

PONTIUS. I know.

She kisses him again.

MARY 1. They would take away my part or worse if they
    knew.

PONTIUS. I will be silent as a dead fish, silent as a closed
    box under water.

*They kiss.
Strange watery noises.*

SCENE 11

The Village Idiot wakes up from a dream, frightened.

VILLAGE IDIOT. Jack! I thought I had me a dream of the Queen. Why, she was standing up in heaven, and she was naked and pregnant – full pregnant, swollen like a melon. Her belly was dangling over her private parts, which were flaming red. They say the privates are the same color as the eyebrows but you never can say with certainty until you've given 'em a thorough look. But I blushed, I did, to see the Queen's privates – they're always covered up with drapes and curtains like a stage. So the Queen, she looks at me, with a real cold glimmer in her eyes like jewels, and she says, "I have come to stop the Passion." And she points her bony little finger at me, and I wake up, breathing heavy and scared-like.

SCENE 12: IN THE FOREST

Mary 1 and Mary 2. The shadows of trees on their faces.

MARY 2. How long?

MARY 1. Too long.

MARY 2. Big?

MARY 1. A little.

MARY 2. In your costume?

MARY 1. Not yet.

MARY 2. Christ.

MARY 1. Yes.

MARY 2. You could be killed.

MARY 1. Don't.

MARY 2. Vomit?

MARY 1. Yes.

MARY 2. Breasts?

MARY 1. Yes. I think so.

MARY 2. Holy mother of God.

MARY 1. Please.

MARY 2. You have to leave.

MARY 1. NO!

MARY 2. What, then?

MARY 1. I want my part.

MARY 2. There's a woman in a neighboring village…

MARY 1. No!

MARY 2. What then, what?

MARY 1. I don't know.

MARY 2. In one month…

MARY 1. I know. But I want my part.

MARY 2. I know you do, Mary.

MARY 1. Please.

Don't tell.

MARY 2. Yes, of course.

MARY 1. The woman in the neighboring village…does she?

MARY 2. Yes.

MARY 1. I'll wait. Two weeks.

MARY 2. I'd like to kill him.

MARY 1. I fear, Mary, sometimes I fear….

MARY 2. What is it?

MARY 1. I dream, night after night, that I give birth to a fish…a huge, ugly, dead fish with a gaping mouth.

SCENE 13: THE FLYING MACHINE

A rehearsal. The Machinist, Director, Mary 1, Mary 2, Carpenter 1 & 2. Carpenter 1 plays the angel Gabriel.

MACHINIST. Our profession is closer to God than any. What is the one power denied to man by God? God gave us fire, God gave us water. We can talk, walk, swim, screw until we're blue in the face. But who wants to swim in the bloody cold water, shivering and stinking like pond scum when you could fly through the tree-tops? But who among us can fly? Huh? Tell me!

And who among us doesn't want to fly? Who among you has never dreamed of flying, of skimming the honey-stalks with your noses? Of flying like water-bugs over ponds and taking in the stench?

But who among us has flown? None! None! And who among us knows how to make a man fly?

Pause.

Me! So shut your bloody traps and listen to me!

I'm going to rig you up by the seat of your pants, and do you know what you're going to do? You are going to fly like a bird like an insect with golden wings like an angel! I've worked with the best of them – I've worked with Simon Daybell, with Martinius Lily, with SEBASTIAN MONK – and none of them – *none* – has ever rigged an angel the way I rig 'em.

Now strap this on.

Carpenter 1 straps on a harness.

VILLAGE IDIOT. *(eyes closed, holding her jack-in-the-box tightly to her chest)* And lo, the angel of the Lord came upon them, and the glory of the Lord shone round about them: and they were sore afraid.

Carpenter 1 shouts as he's rigged up the machine.

THE MACHINIST. Shut your mouth, will you? Do angels scream when they fly? No, by Christ, they like flying! They bloody love it!

Carpenter 1 dangles. Mary 1, meanwhile, looks ill.

DIRECTOR. *(to Carpenter 1)* There. Now say the bloody line.
  And you, *(points to Carpenter 2, who is dressed as Joseph)*
  Kneel down. Look surprised.

Carpenter 2 looks surprised.

Not surprised like you've wet yourself. Surprised as in
amazed. Surprised holy-like. Surprised like your wife's
bosom has grown big as two pumpkins, all at once.

Carpenter 2 opens his mouth wide.

There. Continue.

CARPENTER 1. *(as Gabriel)*	THE VILLAGE IDIOT.
Hail, thou that art highly f-favored, the Lord is with thee, Mary. Bb-lessed art thou among women.	Hail, thou that art highly favored, the Lord is with thee, JACK. Blessed art thou among women.

DIRECTOR. *(to Mary 1)* What's wrong with you? Look surprised. Look happy. Look radiant.

MARY 1. Yes, sir.

DIRECTOR. Joseph – let's have your line.

CARPENTER 2. She is with child, I know not how.
  Who could trust any woman now?
  Hail, Mary!

MARY 1. By God's will, Joseph, must it be.
  For certainly save God and ye
  I know no other man
  Nor in flesh have been defiled.
  God knows all my doing.

CARPENTER 1.	THE VILLAGE IDIOT.
Behold, M-Mary, thou shalt	Behold, Jack, thou shalt

b-bring forth a son	bring forth a son
and shalt call his name	and shalt call his name
J-Jesus.	JACK.

The Sky Turns Red.
Everyone looks up.
The Machinist loses hold of the flying machine.

CARPENTER 1. Oh, the sky!

Carpenter 1's harness falls and he comes crashing down.
He screams.

SCENE 14: MARY VISITS PONTIUS AT WORK

Pontius stands at a counter and guts fish. Sees Mary 1. Drops his work. Washes the fish blood off his hands with water from a bucket.

PONTIUS. You.

MARY 1. I need to speak with you.

PONTIUS. I wrote you letters. I scented them with rose-water.

MARY 1. Where there are no ears.

PONTIUS. What of my letters? Did you get them? Your eyes hard like flint, Mary, you're killing me –

MARY 1. I said I need to speak with you.

PONTIUS. Come to tell me I smell of fish? We rolled into the earth, Mary. Come to tell me you forgot?

MARY 1. I'm pregnant.

PONTIUS. Oh, God.

MARY 1. And don't take the Lord's name in vain, neither.

PONTIUS. Run away with me, Mary. We'll be a Trinity. You, me, the baby. You can nail me to a cross, Mary, I'm yours, yours forever. You can scourge me every night and still I'm yours forever.

She doesn't speak.

Can I touch?

She nods. Pontius puts his hand on her belly, reverent.

My life in your belly! Oh, it's ticking, Mary! I can hear it!

Marry me. Marry everything – the fish-guts, the bile – I'll become clean for you, Mary.

MARY 1. No.

He takes his hand off her stomach.

PONTIUS. You love him, don't you? That it?

MARY 1. I want to keep my part.

PONTIUS. Curse the part, Mary! Curse the part! It's a tiddling, priddling, little turd of a play. Plays aren't real. Your knee on my chest, Mary, that's real. Marry me!

MARY 1. Ever since I was little I've wanted to play the Virgin Mary.

PONTIUS. You can pretend you're the Virgin Mary in my bed! You can scream ten Hail Marys in the ecstasies of love. Do you remember how you shuddered?

MARY 1. Christ won't love me.

PONTIUS. Which one, Mary? My cousin or the one from the good book?

MARY 1. Just Christ, Christ himself...

PONTIUS. By Christ Himself, then, let's run off together – you can have your baby in a manger, the softest hay, your face – honeyed – eyes milky, I'll comb your hair with straw... Kiss me, Mary.

MARY 1. No.

PONTIUS. Leave my sight or I swear...I won't be accountable.

She turns to leave. Turns back.

MARY 1. My wedding dress would turn red.

PONTIUS. What?

MARY. Dresses – they know things – you think they don't – they hang so quietly, but they know things the way you know things and I know things and they tell – oh, yes.

She looks at him, turns and leaves.
Pontius slams his knife down into the table.

SCENE 15: MARY AND MARY

MARY 2. I have an idea.

MARY 1. Tell me.

Mary 2 whispers into Mary 1's ear.

SCENE 16: AT THE CONFESSIONAL

MARY 1. There's been a miracle, Father, I wanted to tell you first. God has impregnated me that I can better play the Virgin Mary.

VISITING FRIAR. Child...

MARY 1. I had a vision, Father. Angels – beautiful angels – calling me, saying, blessed is the fruit of thy womb.

VISITING FRIAR. Sweet Jesus.

MARY 1. I was sleeping, but they called to me from the window...There was one angel, dressed all in blue, with stars in her hair...I felt my belly, and it's become round like a melon since yesterday...

VISITING FRIAR. You're quite sure, Mary?

MARY 1. Yes.

VISITING FRIAR. Glory be to God. A miracle.

He crosses himself.

MARY 1. I feel very honored, of course.

VISITING FRIAR. Never, Mary, never have you...

MARY 1. No, Father, of course not.

VISITING FRIAR. Are you sure, Mary? Blessedly sure?

MARY 1. Yes.

SCENE 17: A REHEARSAL – THE DEATH OF PONTIUS PILATE

Pontius, the Director, the Machinist, Mary 2 and Carpenter 2.

MACHINIST. *(as the Emperor, LOUD)* Out on thee, thou rascally fellow!

Thou hast killed Jesus,

My dear Lord.

DIRECTOR. Remember – you are an emperor. Do you know what that means? Being the emperor means someone else chews your very food for you. No need to shout. Peasants bend forward to hear you whisper. Carry on.

MACHINIST. *(whispering)* Put this fellow in a dungeon to rot,

That he may see no light at all;

he is a sorcerer.

DIRECTOR. Let's move on. Go ahead, Pontius. Now – you are very distressed in this scene.

PONTIUS. I well know I shall die:

Great is my anxiety *(pronounced to rhyme)*

Distressed am I.

DIRECTOR. Use this knife.

The Director gives Pontius a knife.

PONTIUS. So that no man in the world may

Give me a cruel death;

My own heart

With my knife I will pierce –

Oh! alas and welaway –

He stabs himself with a stage knife.
He dies a long, painful stage death, groaning.
He punctures his eyes, slits open his belly.

DIRECTOR. Good, Pontius. You're improving nicely.

The Visiting Friar enters.

VISITING FRIAR. There's been a miracle. Mary is with child.

Pontius gives the Visiting Friar a wild look.
A tableau.

SCENE 18: MARY IS VISITED BY JESUS

Mary 1 lies in bed. John enters, kneels at her bedside.

JOHN. Bless you, Mary.

MARY 1. No, John, no.

JOHN. A miracle sleeps in your belly.

MARY 1. If anything were to happen to me, would you raise the child? Be its father?

JOHN. Anything for you and the child, Mary.

MARY 1. You believe me, don't you?

JOHN. I would never doubt your word, Mary, or the word of the Lord. You're beautiful. You're radiant with the sweat of the Lord on your brow.

MARY 1. I feel it kicking. God's child.

A pause.

JOHN. Marry me. Be my wife. We'll raise the child together as Mary and Joseph did before us. I'll be a good husband, Mary. I'll never touch you, if that's what you want. I'll fish all day – I'll feed us with fruit from the sea.

MARY 1. Oh God, that I could, John.

JOHN. I understand, Mary, if you don't fancy me. I'm not worthy of you...you have God in your belly.

MARY 1. It's not that...It's only that...I'm God's bride now.

JOHN. I see...It's better that way. It's – a miracle.

SCENE 19: THE SCOURGING – A REHEARSAL

Mary 2, Carpenter 1, Carpenter 2 , the Machinist and Pontius.

CARPENTER 2. I see where her eye wanders...She's a pretty little thing, too pretty if you ask me.

CARPENTER 1. St-stop. G-god wouldn't like you to speak that way of Ma-mary.

CARPENTER 2. She's been hankering after John the Fisherman all month and perhaps she's finally gotten what she wanted out of him.

MARY 2. *(to Carpenter 2)* I've seen your lecherous eyes... You wish you could lay a hand on Mary and now she's God's bride you're jealous.

CARPENTER 2. True enough, I'd like to take Miss Mary to a field somewhere, but what does that have to do with the price of eggs and butter? So would every other young lad in this town, and that's *exactly* what I'm saying.

PONTIUS. I'll bloody your face, Simon, if you don't shut your gob!

CARPENTER 2. I never believed the tale in the Good Book anyhow. Mary was probably some young wench knocked up by another bloke, couldn't stand to tell her husband to be – afraid he'd beat her pulpy. Any girl who can persuade the multitudes that God's the father of her bastard child –

Carpenter 1 punches Carpenter 2 in the face. They start brawling.
Enter John the Fisherman, in a loin cloth.

JOHN. What's this! Ho! Hey! Stop the fighting between brothers. Stop! Haven't you heard the news? A miracle in our little town...you should bow your heads and be grateful.

They look down, ashamed.

JOHN. A new Christ is to be born, as the Good Book prophesizes. No longer will I have to play the part of Christ. Mary is with child.

CARPENTER 2. We've heard.

JOHN. Then why all the brawling? Blood trickles down your chin, good brother.

No one speaks. Enter the Director.

DIRECTOR. What's all this? Take up your whips. We've only one week left of rehearsal – where's Mary?

JOHN. I left her home, sick with women's sickness. A glorious sickness to bear for the new Christ.

DIRECTOR. Hmmph. She'll be fined two shillings for missing rehearsal.

JOHN. You cannot fine a woman for bearing the Messiah, with all due respect sir.

DIRECTOR. Very well. Perhaps under the circumstances. Everyone to their places. Mary, you read both parts. Pontius, let's have your speech.

PONTIUS. *(as Pilate)* That I am innocent of this bloode shall ye see;
Both my hands shall weshen be.

Pontius washes his hands.

DIRECTOR. Start whipping.

The chorus pretends to whip John the Fisherman.

Lamentation!

MARY 2. *(as the Virgin Mary)* Why? Why is my son slayn?

A tableau.

SCENE 20: JOHN AND PONTIUS

After rehearsal.

PONTIUS. You think she's God's bride, do you?

JOHN. I see God in her eyes, yes.

PONTIUS. When the baby comes out, I'll wager it'll look less like God and more like me.

JOHN. What?

PONTIUS. You heard me.

John the Fisherman looks at Pontius.
Mary 1's face, illuminated in a window.
A brief tableau.

SCENE 21: MARY AND MARY

The forest.
Mary 2 walks out and meets Mary 1.

MARY 1. I hear them whispering underground, in the trees
– I hear them calling me a whore…

MARY 2. Don't listen. I love you, Mary. Let's run off together.
I'll protect you. We'll raise the child together as Mary
and Joseph did before us. I'll dress as a man…I look
enough like a man…we'll go far away from here.

MARY 1. You don't look a bit like a man, Mary.

MARY 2. What does it matter? Then I won't dress as a man.
I'll dress as myself, but we'll go far, far away.

MARY 1. I have to leave alone, and where I'm going, no one
can follow me.

MARY 2. Mary.

MARY 1. I'm a whore, Mary.

MARY 2. I would follow you anywhere, Mary.

MARY 1. No, dear. Please.

Good-bye.

Mary 1 turns to leave, but before she goes, kisses Mary 2
full on the lips.
Mary 1 leaves.
The Sky Turns Red.

MARY 2. Oh, the sky! Again, the sky!

SCENE 22: THE TOWN SQUARE

The Village Idiot with her jack-in-the-box.

VILLAGE IDIOT. Mary not in her costume
Mary not at home.
Mary not in the lamb white days
Mary, Mary gone.

Do you know, Jack, that a woman's long hair is the last thing to float in the water? It floats, Jack, dry like a lily pad, until in one great rush it goes under – whoosh. Oh, and the fish they wept, Jack, I knew something was wrong – they cried all night and the sea bulged over the earth.

The Visiting Friar and the Director enter.

VISITING FRIAR. God has spoken with me. And God wants you to stop the Passion.

DIRECTOR. But Father, months of work...

VISITING FRIAR. It cannot be right, with Mary nowhere to be found. There's something strange, foreboding, in the whole business.

DIRECTOR. Which is precisely why the play must go on! We made a pact with God, when the plague had eaten the very stomach out of our village, that we would play the Passion and all for the glory of God. If we refuse, I believe that something horrible will visit our town... already, the sky is red.

VISITING FRIAR. But who's to play Mary?

They both look at the Village Idiot.

DIRECTOR. What do you say, dearie, would you like to take part in the play?

THE VILLAGE IDIOT. *(laughing, to Jack)* Jack, would I like to take part in the play?
(She listens to Jack.) What, Jack? I can't hear you.
(to the Director, very serious) Yes, I would like to take part in the play.

SCENE 23: THE PASSION

A bell rings.
John the Fisherman kneels in a pool of light.
Pontius watches, in the shadows.

JOHN. Please, God, let me play the Christ well. Dear Lord, bless Mary. Please let her find her way home.

Crosses himself.

Amen.

PONTIUS. So help me God I'll kill him. I'll drive the nails in deep.

SCENE 24: THE PLAY

EVERYONE. Please lift up your hearts to behold the Holy Passion Play.

Trumpets. A tableau of The Garden of Eden.
John the Fisherman plays Adam and the Village Idiot plays Eve.
Pontius plays the snake.

JOHN. *(as Adam)* Ah! Eve! Thou art to blame!
    On my knees I do here sink!
    Against you I do exclaim
    For I am naked as I think!

VILLAGE IDIOT. *(as Eve)* Alas, Adam, right naked so am I.
    Ah, wicked worm!

She points to his privates.
Then she points to the snake.

JOHN.

So that God will not see
our privates
and stare
We shall cover ourselves
with fig leaves
For we are naked and
bare.

VILLAGE IDIOT.

So that God will not see
our privates
and stare
We shall cover ourselves
with fig leaves
For we are NAKED –
and all bare!

John covers himself with a fig leaf.
He then covers the Village Idiot with a fig leaf.
Suddenly, the arrival of Queen Elizabeth's courtiers, played by the Carpenters. Trumpets. Fanfare.
A murmur goes through the audience.

COURTIERS. The Queen has blessed your little town with her presence.

A louder murmur goes through the audience.
Queen Elizabeth walks onto the stage, waving.
The players bow their heads low to the ground.

THE QUEEN. My loving people.

Do you know, when they place me in my golden coffer, what they will find? They will scrape at my face with a jeweled pen-knife, and they will discover layer upon layer of white paint. A wall of paint as thick as this joint, in my thumb. They will be surprised. They will open their eyes wide. They do not know that Queens do not wash, and that Queens are obliged to paint their faces so that Queens do not appear to become old or ugly.

I do not want the gravediggers to scrape white paint off the dead faces of my subjects. I want my subjects to remain clean. Clean and honest and loyal to the crown. I do not want my subjects to impersonate the holy figure of Christ.

Did Christ paint his face?

No! Such things are unholy. If any man or woman in England is seen with a painted face, assuming the person of a holy figure on a stage, I will have them beheaded. Immediately.

COURTIERS. The Queen has spoken.

She turns to go. The players raise their heads slightly to watch her go.
The Queen moves to exit. She stops in her tracks.

Is any house in this village concealing a priest?

My subjects should feel free to confess all of their sins to me.

No one speaks.
She walks among her people, slowing as she walks past the Visiting Friar.

HAS ANYONE IN THIS VILLAGE ANYTHING TO CONFESS?

No one speaks.

Good. I'll have my courtiers search your houses. Just to be certain.

The Queen exits with her entourage to loud fanfare.
The players are silent. They exit, one by one, collecting their props.

SCENE 25: JOHN THE FISHERMAN'S KITCHEN

JOHN. Where will you go?

VISITING FRIAR. To France. Until it is safe for priests in England – when a bastard head of state is severed from its body.

JOHN. I don't understand you, Good Friar.

VISITING FRIAR. Good. When they come, asking questions, you can say truly: I've no idea. I only made the man some eggs. Do you have anything to confess before I go?

JOHN. Perhaps there is something. I believe I liked it a little too well, playing the role of Christ.

VISITING FRIAR. God be with you.

JOHN. And with you.

SCENE 26: THE TOWN SQUARE

The Director, Carpenter 1, Carpenter 2, Pontius, MARY
2, the Machinist and the Village Idiot.
One by one, the players hand in their costumes to the
Director.
They are sad.
The Machinist hands in his emperor costume.

DIRECTOR. We can get five shillings for this. No, seven –
that's fine material, good stitching.

Mary 2 hands in her costume.

Eight for this.

Mary 2 holds Mary 1's halo.

MARY 2. May I keep this?

DIRECTOR. I'll wager the professional acting companies in
London have no need for halos. Keep it. Only hide it.

Carpenter 1 hands in his costume, angel wings.

This one's damaged.

CARPENTER 1. From flying.

DIRECTOR. Throw it out.

Suddenly, John the Fisherman enters with the body of
Mary 1.
She is dripping wet.
Water pours out of her mouth onto the stage.
Water continues to pour out of her and off of her.
Everyone turns to look in horror.

JOHN. I fished her out of the sea –

John lays the body down.
A tableau.

SCENE 27: THE DEATH OF PONTIUS

The sky is red.
Pontius, by the body of Mary 1, holds a knife.
John the Fisherman is fishing on the other side of the
stage, as if in a dream.

PONTIUS. No more bloody play, Mary.

You needn't have drowned yourself, dear.

My cousin is beside himself. He's out in the boat fishing.

The fish drink up his salty tears.

The moon is cradled by the night – the curved white slipper of the moon, reclining, rocked back into the night, will rock me to sleep. Mary, the doctor who birthed me, see, he didn't sew up my belly properly. My belly is an open wound and the air – she smites it. There is nothing left for me, Mary, but to find you. I will swim to you, arms outstretched.

So that no man in the world may
Give me a cruel death;
My own heart
With my knife I will pierce –
Oh, alas, and welaway –

He stabs himself with a knife. He closes his eyes. Drums.
Big beautiful fish puppets surround him, lift him up,
and carry him offstage. The sky turns blue.

Intermission

PASSION PLAY

PART TWO

Oberammergau, Bavaria, 1934

CHARACTERS

FOOT SOLDIER . . . . .plays Pontius Pilate
(was Pontius the Fish Gutter in Part One)

ERIC. . . . . plays Jesus
(was John the Fisherman in Part One)

ELSA. . . . . .plays the Virgin Mary
(was Mary 1 in Part One)

MARY 2 . . . . plays Mary Magdalen
(was Mary 2 in Part One)

THE VISITING ENGLISHMAN. . . . . . (was Visiting Friar in Part One)
or **SIMON LILY**

VIOLET . . . . .dressed as a normal girl
(was Village Idiot in Part One)

CARPENTER 1 . . . . also plays ensemble roles and bird
or **JOHANN**   (was Carpenter 1 in Part One)

CARPENTER 2. . . . . .also plays ensemble roles
or **LUDWIG**   (was Carpenter 2 in Part One)

DIRECTOR. . . . . (was Director in Part One)
or **ROCHUS SHALLHAMMER**

GERMAN OFFICER. . . . . (was Machinist in Part One)

HITLER . . . . (was Queen Elizabeth in Part One)

SET

The suggestion of a forest.
A playing space.

SCENE 1: PROLOGUE

CHORUS.

> Oberammergau, 1934!
> The Passion Play's three hundred year anniversary.
> Special Passion Play trains –
> One-third the usual cost!

> Visit the Oberammergau Carving Shop.
> Crucifixes of every style. Made to Order.
> Cheapest Prices. Good Service.

> Visit our biggest hotel. Exceptionally hygienic.
> Near the woods and free from dust.
> Price, out of Passion season, 4 marks.
> Price, during Passion season, 12 marks.

The sound of a train whistle.

SCENE 2

The Visiting Englishman is writing a letter.
Violet sits nearby, playing with a white ribbon.

VISITING ENGLISHMAN.
Second of April, 1934.

Dearest Harriet,

Oberammergau is certainly quaint. A more friendly
and peaceful place could hardly be found in Europe.
There is, of course, quite a lot of Catholic supersti-
tion here – they certainly do not have a very complex
understanding of the relation between art and life.
Today, as I wandered through the town square, I saw
the most remarkable little girl crying slow, medieval
tears.

"What's the matter?" I asked.

*The Visiting Englishman leaves off his letter-writing to
enact the scene.*

VIOLET. I haven't a part. A part in the play. I would so love to
be in the play. But only the natives of Oberammergau
have parts.

VISITING ENGLISHMAN. That doesn't seem fair.

VIOLET. Fair's fair. I am an outsider and haven't the look of
an Oberammergauer.

VISITING ENGLISHMAN. And what is the look of the Oberammergauer?

VIOLET. To be jolly and fat.

VISITING ENGLISHMAN. And you are not so very jolly.

VIOLET. No.

VISITING ENGLISHMAN. And what's your name, my dear?

VIOLET. They call me the village idiot.

VISITING ENGLISHMAN. Surely that's not your name?

VIOLET. No. My name means Violet in another language.
The children here can't pronounce it. So they call me
the village idiot.

SCENE 4

Eric and the Foot Soldier. Day.

ERIC. When will you leave? Do they tell you?

FOOT SOLDIER. Soon.

ERIC. Won't you be homesick?

FOOT SOLDIER. I'll have the whole world to entertain me.

ERIC. And you'll leave even if it means not playing Pontius Pilate?

FOOT SOLDIER. Plays aren't real. The soldier's boot – that's real.

ERIC. I should like to come with you.

FOOT SOLDIER. The Christus cannot come with the soldier. The Christus must stay behind.

ERIC. I'm tired of crucifixions.

FOOT SOLDIER. You are?

ERIC. My arms are tired. I was on the cross for four hours yesterday, rehearsing. I tried to raise a cup of water to my mouth and couldn't, I was shaking so badly.

FOOT SOLDIER. I could rub them.

ERIC. All right.

The Foot Soldier rubs Eric's arms.

FOOT SOLDIER. Let's play a game. It's called would you rather.

ERIC. All right.

FOOT SOLDIER. Would you rather be a just beggar or an unjust king?

ERIC. A just beggar. The pangs of conscience are worse than the pangs of hunger.

FOOT SOLDIER. I should have known you were one of those.

ERIC. Well, what would you rather?

FOOT SOLDIER. An unjust king, of course. The pangs of conscience are barely audible when the stomach is growling. Would you rather be a dwarf or a hermaphrodite?

ERIC. A dwarf, I suppose.

FOOT SOLDIER. For all the world to see your shame?

ERIC. My turn. Would you rather be a mediocre composer whose name was remembered for centuries, or a glorious composer lost to obscurity?

FOOT SOLDIER. A glorious composer lost to obscurity, of course. You?

ERIC. The same! Would you rather be Christ or Pontius Pilate?

FOOT SOLDIER. Pontius Pilate.

ERIC. Why?

FOOT SOLDIER. Very unpleasant, the nails, the whipping, the blood… No one actually wants to *be* Christ, they only want to admire him from a distance.

ERIC. That's not a very nice thing to say.

FOOT SOLDIER. But it's true. My turn. Would you rather be me or you?

ERIC. That's a strange question.

FOOT SOLDIER. Go on.

ERIC. Let's see…if I were you I would take everything as a joke – I would get drunk to forget my troubles and I would have the most interesting, intelligent eyes. No one would know me but everyone would like me. If I were me, I would be – timid. I would take little bites of food and fall in love with the wrong people.

FOOT SOLDIER. You still haven't answered the question.

ERIC. I would rather be you in the evening and I would rather be me in the morning.

FOOT SOLDIER. Why?

ERIC. I could soak myself with pleasure in the evening and not remember in the morning. And you – would you rather be me or you?

FOOT SOLDIER. I would rather be me in wartime and you in peacetime.

ERIC. Why is that?

FOOT SOLDIER. I couldn't carry a gun properly if I had your little hands.

ERIC. Little! I don't have little hands –

He holds his hands up to the Foot Soldier's hands.

FOOT SOLDIER. You know what they say about the size of a man's hands.

ERIC. No.

FOOT SOLDIER. Think about it. If you have big hands, maybe other things will be big.

Eric takes his hand away.

ERIC. Gloves?

FOOT SOLDIER. Don't act stupid. You know what I'm talking about.

ERIC. You have a perverse imagination.

FOOT SOLDIER. We could compare. It's important to know these things.

ERIC. I have rehearsal.

FOOT SOLDIER. Not for another hour.

ERIC. I don't know my lines.

FOOT SOLDIER. All right, all right, I'll stop bothering you. You want a cigarette?

ERIC. Okay.

The Foot Soldier gives Eric a cigarette.
Eric puffs on it without sophistication.

FOOT SOLDIER. Here – hold it like this – that's better. That's how they hold cigarettes in Berlin.

ERIC. How would you know?

FOOT SOLDIER. I've seen pictures.

ERIC. I have to memorize my lines.

FOOT SOLDIER. Should I test you?

ERIC. Okay.

FOOT SOLDIER. Art thou the King of the Jews?

Pause. Eric doesn't remember his line.

Art thou the King of the Jews?

ERIC. Ahh…Dost thou say this of thine own accord – or – or –

FOOT SOLDIER. *(giving him the line)* Or – have – others…

ERIC. …said it of me?

FOOT SOLDIER. Good.

(performing) Am I a Jew? Thine own people handed thee over to me. They say that thou wouldst make thyself King of the Jews.

ERIC. My kingdom is of –

FOOT SOLDIER. Not –

ERIC. My kingdom is *not* of this world.

FOOT SOLDIER. Thou art a king then!

ERIC. Thou sayest so.

FOOT SOLDIER. What is the truth?

Pause.

ERIC. I'm sorry. I can't concentrate. Every time I say my lines I think of my father watching me and my mind goes blank.

FOOT SOLDIER. Your father was an old man playing the Christ. You're a young man. You need to play *that* Christ – a leader of men – a leader of nations –

ERIC. I'd rather play Judas. To be hated, that's easy. To be loved – that's hard.

FOOT SOLDIER. You need to relax. Have more fun. We'll go mushroom hunting this afternoon.

ERIC. I should sit with my father – he's been getting worse.

FOOT SOLDIER. Come on. A nice tender mushroom… picked with your own hands…

ERIC. Well – all right. I shouldn't let you go all by yourself. You're a horrible judge of mushrooms.

SCENE 5

The Visiting Englishman interviews Mary 2, outside her father's sickroom.

VISITING ENGLISHMAN. I have once heard it said that one can measure the degree to which a village is civilized by the variety of fungi it eats.

MARY 2. Oberammergau has all kinds of mushrooms.

VISITING ENGLISHMAN. Does it?

MARY 2. Oh, yes! Only you have to be careful. Some mushrooms, when broken apart, spread through and through with beautiful reds and unearthly greens. But secretly, they're poisonous.

VISITING ENGLISHMAN. Are they deadly?

MARY 2. Oh, yes.

VISITING ENGLISHMAN. I suppose I'd better stay out of the forest then.

MARY 2. Oh – but Oberammergau has the most beautiful forests in Bavaria!

VISITING ENGLISHMAN. Well, then, perhaps I'd better take my jaunts in the forest but defer to the native's superior judgment in the art of distinguishing between mushrooms. *(He laughs.)*

MARY 2. *(She does not laugh.)* That's a good idea.
    Why have you come to our town?

VISITING ENGLISHMAN. Actually, I'm writing a book on the theater.

MARY 2. Really? A whole book!

VISITING ENGLISHMAN. Well, yes. Do you mind if I ask you some questions?

MARY 2. Please.

VISITING ENGLISHMAN. Is it true that your father plays the role of Christ in the Passion?

MARY 2. Not this year. Father is too old, so they gave the part to my brother, which is, of course, a great honor.

VISITING ENGLISHMAN. Was your father disappointed when he heard the news?

MARY 2. Oh, yes. He took ill the very next day.

VISITING ENGLISHMAN. And how did you feel, as a little girl, watching your father play the Christus?

MARY 2. I hated to see his side pierced and the blood running out. I confess I had to stop myself from crying out. I wanted with all my heart to run onstage and fight the Jews. I could not understand why all the people watching did nothing.

VISITING ENGLISHMAN. Your father has quite a reputation as a holy man.

MARY 2. Oh, yes. When father and I walked together through the forests, Christ would walk with us.

VISITING ENGLISHMAN. Right.

MARY 2. Father had many offers from America to come play parts in New York City. But he preferred to stay here.

VISITING ENGLISHMAN. I'm afraid your father's genius would be lost on Americans. The only art Americans understand is the big red painting that matches the big red rug on their living room floor.

He laughs.

MARY 2. I don't know – I'm afraid I've never been to America. If you'll excuse me, I should give Father his supper.

THE VISITING ENGLISHMAN. May I take his picture before I go?

MARY 2. I'm sorry, but Papa doesn't pose for pictures.

SCENE 6: A REHEARSAL

The Visiting Englishman takes pictures.
Eric rushes in late.

DIRECTOR. CHRIST TEARS DOWN THE TEMPLE! Begin!

ERIC. What – what do I see here? Is this God's house? Or is it naught but – naught to you but –

MARY 2. What is wrong with you?

ERIC. *(whispering to Mary 2)* I can't remember my lines…

MARY 2. You were supposed to practice them this afternoon! Where were you?

ERIC. In the forest –

DIRECTOR. *(to Eric, giving lines)* Or is it naught to you but a market-place?

ERIC. Or is it naught to you but a market-place? You dishonor the abode of my Father. You – money-changers –

Violet enacts her own play to compete with the other play, which she doesn't like.

VIOLET. I don't like that story.
How about – once upon a time there
were children named Hansel
and Gretel.

DIRECTOR. Shut up, village idiot. Jewish chorus, your lines!

THE JEWISH CHORUS. My money, ah, my money! Who will restore this loss to me?

DIRECTOR. *(to Eric)* Push the vessel this time! Again!

Eric pushes over a vessel of money and the Jewish Chorus picks up the gold coins.

VIOLET. Hansel and Gretel ate delicious candies off an old witch's house.

JEWISH CHORUS. My money, ah, my money!

VIOLET. DIRECTOR. Release the doves!

Eric opens a bird cage and two doves fly out.

JEWISH CHORUS. My doves!

VIOLET. The birds ate up
    their breadcrumbs.
    When people are chasing
    you through the forest
    Don't rely on breadcrumbs.

ERIC. Away from here, Servants of Mammon! I bid you go!
    Take what is yours, and leave this holy place!

CARPENTER 1. *(as Jewish Chorus)* What b-boastful insolent
    talk!

DIRECTOR. Again. Try not to stutter this time.

CARPENTER 1. *(as Jewish Chorus)* What b-boastful insolent
    talk.

DIRECTOR. See me privately after rehearsal, Johann. We
    need to discuss the renewal of your contract.

CARPENTER 1. Yes, sir.

VIOLET. Then the old witch wanted to starve Hansel –
    but Hansel was smart to put a
    little bone outside of his
    cage to look like a finger –

DIRECTOR. I said, shut your mouth village idiot! Continue!

ERIC. Do not destroy this temple –
    No – Destroy this temple –

VIOLET. One day, the witch got
    hungry and said, Hansel,
    I'm going to cook you in
    the oven!

DIRECTOR. Your lines!
    Destroy this temple, and in three days
    I will raise it up again!

VIOLET. *(to Eric)* Hansel was scared.
    Wouldn't you be scared?
    If someone wanted to push
    you in an oven?

ERIC. Destroy this temple, and I
    will, I will –

VIOLET. But then Hansel pushed
the *witch* into the oven.
He said, with your fat bottom,
you'd make a better dinner!

DIRECTOR. I said, shut your mouth, village idiot!

VIOLET. And the witch screamed
from inside the oven, like
this, AAAAAAAAAAAH!

DIRECTOR. *(moving to Violet)* I said, shut your mouth! The
only people who should be speaking in this rehearsal
are the people with parts in the play. Do you have a
part in this play?

VIOLET. No, sir.

DIRECTOR. Then I suggest you practice being silent. Do
you know how to be silent?

Violet opens her mouth to speak.

Don't answer me – only nod.

Violet nods.

Good. Because if children do not learn how to be
silent, the world will teach them. Do you understand?
Don't answer me – only nod.

She nods.

Let's move on to the Jewish High Council, Scene 3.
Caiaphas, you stand here. Take it from: "All moves
excellently well, worthy Fathers."

CARPENTER 2. *(as Caiaphas)* All moves excellently well,
worthy Fathers. Now: what shall we do with this Jesus
of Nazareth, once He is delivered into our hands?

CARPENTER 2. *(as Rabbi)* Let Him be thrown into the deep-
est, darkest dungeon, and kept there! Let Him go
through a living death!

DIRECTOR. Very good, Johann.

CARPENTER 2. *(as Caiaphas)* No. He must die! Until He dies
there is no peace in Israel, no safety for the Law of
Moses!

DIRECTOR. Try your lower register for the first line, and work your way up to the end of the speech.

CARPENTER. *(better acting)* No. He must die! Until He dies there is no peace in Israel, no safety for the Law of Moses!

DIRECTOR. Yes – I think that'll work.

SCENE 7

Elsa alone in her dressing room, looking in the mirror.
Enter the German Officer. Her face changes.

GERMAN OFFICER. You were a very pretty picture at rehearsal. Were those real tears?

ELSA. An actress doesn't give away her secrets.

GERMAN OFFICER. You are very cruel. Would you wash my feet, Elsa, the way you wash the feet of Christ?

ELSA. Your feet might smell from being stuck in those big black boots all day.

GERMAN OFFICER. You're like a sphinx, Elsa. You should be in the moving pictures.

ELSA. Please, sir.

GERMAN OFFICER. I have a very pretty house, in a very pretty forest, with very pretty pewter mugs. I have a lamp shade from the Kaiser himself. I fly small, fast planes all over the world. But upon my return, there is no one to sit at my table and smile sweetly.

ELSA. Lamp shades don't make for very good company.

GERMAN OFFICER. They say that the Marys of Oberammergau do not marry because they want to keep their parts. I hope you are not one of the foolish ones, Elsa.

ELSA. Do I look foolish?

GERMAN OFFICER. No.

ELSA. I have now refused three men all for the dream of playing Mary. All of them now settled into clean little homes with clean little wives, not half so pretty as I am. There is an old saying about a woman who goes searching for sticks in the forest. She passes by many sticks because she wants to find the straightest one. By the time she reaches the edge of the forest, only crooked sticks are left. Do you understand me?

GERMAN OFFICER. A smile like that would make any man want to *misunderstand* you.

He moves in to kiss her. She stops him.

ELSA. A man who has the milk for free will not buy the cow, sir.

GERMAN OFFICER. You speak of sticks and cows. I am a blunt man, Elsa. Will you ever marry?

ELSA. Is that a proposal, sir?

GERMAN OFFICER. Is that a yes?

ELSA. I wish to play Mary one last time. And after –

GERMAN OFFICER. After?

ELSA. Perhaps –

GERMAN OFFICER. A man cannot live on perhaps.

ELSA. But there are many kinds of perhaps – perhaps you *can* live on perhaps –

GERMAN OFFICER. Perhaps like this?

He slides his hand up her dress.

ELSA. Perhaps –

He slides his hand further.
She smiles.

ELSA. But no one must know –

GERMAN OFFICER. Oh, Elsa.

She puts a finger to her lips.
He grabs her.

SCENE 8: NIGHT

Mary 2 and Eric at home. Eric is reading a book.

MARY 2. What are you reading?

ERIC. Nothing.

She snatches his book – a volume of Rilke.

MARY 2. Oooh – poetry! Since when do you like poetry? Rose, oh pure contradiction, joy of being….

ERIC. Don't! Put it down.

She puts the book down.

MARY 2. Sorry. Who gave it to you? The foot soldier?

ERIC. None of your business.

MARY 2. Do you like it?

ERIC. The book?

MARY 2. What else?

ERIC. Yes, I like it.

MARY 2. Well, I've never understood poetry.

ERIC. Your loss.

MARY 2. I often think that people who write books are stupid, solitary people. They begin as sickly children, with no friends, so they make books into friends. But they don't write books to befriend lonely children – no – out of their bitterness they write books to make men lonely.

ERIC. I want to leave, Mary.

MARY 2. What?

ERIC. I want to leave…I want to join something…bigger than myself…bigger than this town…I always thought I wanted to play the Christus. Well, I don't believe in plays anymore. The soldier's boot – that's real. The life of the soldier – there's something.

MARY 2. You should be honored to play your part. Father is dying, all for the loss of the Christus, and you spouting this!

ERIC. I want to see the world.

MARY 2. This isn't the world?

ERIC. No, this isn't the world! I want to see steam engines and skyscrapers and great big opera houses.

MARY 2. You want to see the underpants of French dancers!

ERIC. Things are happening in the world, Mary. Exciting things. They're building a new Germany – there's hope for the future and jobs for everyone –

MARY 2. You have a job.

ERIC. Carving crucifixes for tourists all day? That's not a job for a man.

MARY 2. And what would you fight for? What did Father fight for? He came back to a dead country with no gold left in its pockets. You should spend more time with Father and less time dreaming of wars that are never going to happen!

ERIC. Let's not fight, Mary.

A silence.

MARY 2. Do you remember when we were little – you stayed home sick from school one day. You were supposed to feed my bird. I said, no matter what, don't let my bird fly outside. You played with the bird. It flew like crazy around the kitchen. You were afraid the bird would fly into the garden so you slammed the kitchen door as the bird was flying out and you killed it. I came home from school and you had the strangest look on your face. What's wrong? I said. Nothing, you said. Then all of a sudden you started crying. I killed your bird, you said. And now no one will ever love me.

ERIC. I remember.

MARY 2. How could a boy like that join the army?

SCENE 9: THE VISITING ENGLISHMAN AND THE DIRECTOR

The Director comes upon the Visiting Englishman, who is startled.

DIRECTOR. I don't know you.

VISITING ENGLISHMAN. I don't suppose we've been introduced, then, have we?

DIRECTOR. No.

VISITING ENGLISHMAN. Simon Lily.

DIRECTOR. Rochus Schallhammer.

VISITING ENGLISHMAN. Ah! The director of the Passion. Delighted.

The Visiting Englishman extends his hand. The Director shakes it, firmly.

DIRECTOR. What brings you to our town?

VISITING ENGLISHMAN. Well, actually, I'm writing a book on the theater.

DIRECTOR. Really. A whole book!

VISITING ENGLISHMAN. Why yes.

DIRECTOR. Maybe you should ask me some questions. An interview. For the book. You know.

VISITING ENGLISHMAN. Well, let's see. I'm quite unprepared, you know. Umm…right. Do you *enjoy* directing the Passion?

DIRECTOR. Yes. I enjoy.

VISITING ENGLISHMAN. Right. Good. Umm… *Why* do you enjoy directing the Passion?

DIRECTOR. I will confess something to you. There are times in every man's life – in his personal life even – when he needs a director. His eyes are muddy. Maybe he has a sty. Maybe his hands are tied. Whatever it is – he can't see – he can't think. He needs someone with vision – me – someone stronger – me – to tell him what to do.

VISITING ENGLISHMAN. Ah, I see. How marvelous.

DIRECTOR. Why don't you write down?

VISITING ENGLISHMAN. Oh, how stupid of me, really. Do you mind repeating yourself?

DIRECTOR. No. I don't mind. There are times in every man's life – in his personal life even – when he needs a director. His eyes are muddy. Maybe he has a sty. Maybe his hands are tied. Whatever it is – he can't see – he can't think. He needs someone with vision – me – someone stronger – me – to tell him what to do.

VISITING ENGLISHMAN. To tell him what to do…there. I believe I've got the whole speech down, Herr Schallhammer. Thank you very much indeed.

DIRECTOR. Not at all. I like to help.

SCENE 10: THE LAST SUPPER – A REHEARSAL.

*Violet hides under the Last Supper table. The cast moves
into the Last Supper tableau. Eric rushes into place, late.*

DIRECTOR. Places, places for the Last Supper!

(*to Eric*) You're late!

MARY 2. (*whispering*) Where were you?

ERIC. Mushroom hunting.

MARY 2. Honestly!

VISITING ENGLISHMAN. (*to Eric*) May I take your photograph?

ERIC. I'd better not – they sell them at the tourist bureau –

The bulb flashes.

VISITING ENGLISHMAN. Oops!

DIRECTOR. (*to Eric*) Your lines!

ERIC. (*Whispering urgently to Mary 2*) Mary, I can't remember
my lines…

MARY 2. What's wrong with you?

VIOLET. (*Whispering to him from under the table*) I have longed
to share this Passover with you before I suffer.

The Director busies himself fixing the tableau.

ERIC. (*Loud and performative*) I have longed to share this
Passover with you before I suffer.

(*whispering to Violet*) Thank you! Do you know the next
bit?

VIOLET. Verily, verily, I say unto you, one of you at this table
will betray me.

ERIC. (*to Violet*) Yes – that's it! Clever girl!

Verily, verily, I say unto you, one of you at this table will
betray me.

DISCIPLES. What! A betrayer amongst us? Impossible!

Eric turns to Violet to see if she knows the next line.

VIOLET.	**ERIC.** *(echoing)*
I *will* forgive sinners	I *will* forgive sinners
but it's probably best not	but it's probably best not
to sin	to sin
in the first place.	in the first place.
You have to admit, some	You have to admit, some
pretty strange things will	pretty strange things will
be done in my name.	be done in my name.
In time,	In time,
you will crawl around	you will crawl around
like	like
pigs snorting in the mud	pigs snorting in the mud
looking for the answer to	looking for the answer to
this fundamental	this fundamental
question:	question:
is there a God?	is there a God?

Eric works himself up into a performative lather.

And if you decide that	And if you decide that
there	there
is no God, will you need	is no God, will you need
someone	someone
with vision, someone	with vision, someone
stronger,	stronger,
to tell you what to do?	to tell you what to do?
Resist,	Resist,
I say unto you!	I say unto you!

Becoming almost simultaneous.

And finally, I want	And finally, I want
everyone	everyone
at this table,	at this table,
eating my blood and my	eating my blood and my
body,	body,
to remember that	to remember that
I am a Jew.	I am a Jew.
Wait. This is not –	

DIRECTOR. What is that voice?

GERMAN OFFICER. The Village Idiot.

The Director pulls Violet out from under the table.

DIRECTOR. I propose that the village idiot be put in this box with no food for one week as punishment for mocking the voice of Christ. All in favor say aye.

ALL. *(with the exception of the Visiting Englishman)* AYE.

The Visiting Englishman flashes a picture.
The Director puts Violet in the empty bird-cage.

VIOLET. If you lock me up, I'll make the sky turn red. Now, now!

She closes her eyes. The sky remains the same.

Did you see that? Did you see?

No one sees.

SCENE 11

Mary 2 and Eric.

MARY 2. How could you forget your lines?

ERIC. I was confused.

MARY 2. You were more than confused! You were stupid. Father says you should pray more. He says if you feel the grace of God, you'll remember the right words.

ERIC. Father says this, Father says that. Why don't you find yourself a husband to boss around.

I'm sorry.

MARY 2. What is *wrong* with you lately?

ERIC. Mary. I've been thinking. When Father played his part, he got this – funny glow on his face, do you remember? Sort of like this…

He demonstrates.

I've been trying to get a glow on my face when I say my part.

MARY 2. Most of the people in the audience will see you from a distance. They will not be able to tell if your face is glowing.

ERIC. I know – but –

MARY 2. And the people in the front row – they paid a lot of *money* to see your face glow – so they will *imagine* that your face is glowing, even if it's not. The important thing is to remember your lines. And to say them. Word for word.

ERIC. But, there's a difference, isn't there? When you do – a thing – and feel – a thing – at the same time?

MARY 2. I don't understand.

ERIC. I mean – when you're playing your part – or other times – have you ever felt – the grace of God pour into you like a fever? So you don't have to – decide – I think this or I think that – suddenly you're bigger than yourself – and you're looking at the clouds – isn't that how it's supposed to feel?

MARY 2. How *what's* supposed to feel?

ERIC. Anything – big – important – love – or – or – art – or
 – marching with hundreds of people –

MARY 2. Are you in love?

ERIC. No!

> *A pause.*
>
> Wait. Did you hear that?
>
> *There was no sound.*

MARY 2. What is it?

ERIC. Go – look in his room –

MARY 2. You.

ERIC. You.

MARY 2. You.

ERIC. No.

MARY 2. Why?

ERIC. I'm afraid.

MARY 2. There's nothing to be afraid of.

ERIC. Then hurry.

> *She looks in their father's room.*
>
> Is he breathing?

MARY 2. I don't think so.

ERIC. My God.

> We have to call a doctor.

MARY 2. What for?

ERIC. But his body…

MARY 2. *(with compassion)* Go see. It's nothing to be frightened of. It's a body. That's all.

SCENE 12

Violet in her box.

VIOLET. A cross is like someone is cross with you so he folds his arms across his chest. A cross is like I cross my heart and hope to die – is like telling the truth, the whole truth and nothing but the truth. A cross is like I'm cross-eyed so I can't see.

Eric enters. He removes his shoes and socks. He goes to the stage, walking through his blocking. She watches him.

Hello.

ERIC. You startled me.

VIOLET. You look sad.

ERIC. I – never mind.

VIOLET. What are you doing?

ERIC. Rehearsing.

VIOLET. In the middle of the night? Which part?

ERIC. It's called The Mount of Olives.

VIOLET. What happens in that part?

ERIC. I ask my disciples to watch with me for an hour. But they fall asleep.

VIOLET. Why?

ERIC. They're tired.

VIOLET. Oh. That sounds like a nice part. I get tired of the bloody parts. I wish there were more miracle parts – making five hundred fish out of one fish. Or walking on water.

ERIC. I suppose it's hard to put on stage – walking on water.

VIOLET. No, they could do it. People like the bloody parts better.

ERIC. Yes, I suppose they do.

You tricked me at rehearsal, didn't you?

VIOLET. I only meant to help.

ERIC. Did you?

VIOLET. Yes.

ERIC. Do you want to get out of that box?

VIOLET. Yes.

Eric lets her out of the box.

VIOLET. Thank you.

ERIC. Now run along and don't tell anyone. Go on now.
Good-night.

She runs off stage.
He remains, in the night.
A large orange moon appears in the sky.
Eric looks at the moon.
The German Officer enters and looks on, unobserved.
The Foot Soldier comes behind Eric, putting his hands
over Eric's eyes.

FOOT SOLDIER. What do you see?

ERIC. The moon is huge – orange and bloody – a laughing
judge – presiding over an orange trial.

The Foot Soldier takes his hands away.

FOOT SOLDIER. Now look. The moon is gold.

ERIC. I'm afraid.

FOOT SOLDIER. What are you afraid of, little Christ?

ERIC. Everything.

FOOT SOLDIER. Perhaps we should switch roles. I don't
want to put you to death.

ERIC. But you have to.

FOOT SOLDIER. What if I refused? What if I saved you
from the mob – took you home with me, bathed your
wounds with warm water?

ERIC. Impossible.

FOOT SOLDIER. Why impossible? You see only the mountain, you must learn to see the sky on the other side.

ERIC. The foot soldier is a dreamer.

FOOT SOLDIER. The Christus has no faith.

They embrace.
The German Officer looks on, unobserved.

SCENE 13

Day. Backstage. The German Officer, Elsa, and the Foot Soldier. Elsa arranges her halo in an imaginary mirror.

GERMAN OFFICER. Oh, Elsa, you look exquisite.

He touches her.

(to the Foot Soldier) Doesn't she?

What do you say, soldier? Cat got your tongue?

FOOT SOLDIER. Yes, sir.

GERMAN OFFICER. The foot soldier does not appreciate women as I do. Soldier, come here!

FOOT SOLDIER. Yes, sir.

GERMAN OFFICER. Place your hand on the Virgin's behind.

FOOT SOLDIER. I'd rather not, sir.

GERMAN OFFICER. It's an order.

The Foot Soldier places his hand on Elsa's behind.

This, soldier, in your hands, is womanly flesh. It feels something like a melon, or a ripe squash. Ripe, deliciously ripe, almost falling from the branch, but not quite fallen. That's what makes it so tantalizing. Understand?

FOOT SOLDIER. Yes, sir.

GERMAN OFFICER. I want you to remember. Repeat after me. This is a woman's flesh.

FOOT SOLDIER. This is a woman's flesh.

GERMAN OFFICER. It feels something like a melon, or a ripe squash.

FOOT SOLDIER. It feels something like a melon, or a ripe squash.

GERMAN OFFICER. How I love womanly flesh.

FOOT SOLDIER. How I love womanly flesh.

GERMAN OFFICER. Soldier, do you know what happens to men in the German army who do not appreciate women the way a man should?

FOOT SOLDIER. I don't know what you mean, sir.

GERMAN OFFICER. Oh, I think you do.

Enter the Visiting Englishman.

VISITING ENGLISHMAN. Knock, knock...Am I interrupting something?

GERMAN OFFICER. No.

VISITING ENGLISHMAN. Well, I suppose everyone's nervous about opening night – got the jitters as they say. I must say, I'm bursting with excitement. You're looking lovely, Elsa.

ELSA. Thank you.

VISITING ENGLISHMAN. Well. I suppose you have to put on your makeup and what not?

ELSA. We don't wear makeup, Mr. Lily.

THE VISITING ENGLISHMAN. Really! I could have sworn you had rouge on your cheeks.

ELSA. Here – come see if you like.

The Visiting Englishman goes to her. He tries to rub the rouge off her cheeks. There is none.

THE VISITING ENGLISHMAN. Remarkable.

ELSA. You see, here in Oberammergau, everything is as it appears to be.

A bell rings, ushering the audience into the theater.

SCENE 14

Eric prays in a pool of light.

ERIC. Dear God, let me play Christ well for the sake of my father. I know I am unworthy of the part. Please forgive my sins – I won't name them – you know them all.

Enter the Director.

DIRECTOR. Get up. Places.

ERIC. Yes, sir.

DIRECTOR. Don't forget your lines today.

ERIC. I won't, sir.

DIRECTOR. Because, if you do, you'll disgrace not only me, but your father, your faith, your village, and your nation. Do you understand me?

ERIC. Yes.

DIRECTOR. Good.

The Director leaves. Eric rehearses to himself, softly.
Mary 2 enters quietly and watches.

ERIC. Many shall come in my name, saying "I am Christ" and shall deceive the multitudes...For false Christs and false prophets shall rise. The sun shall be darkened, and the moon shall not give her light...Take heed. Watch and pray; lest coming suddenly He find you sleeping. And this is what I say unto all: watch.

MARY 2. You remembered your lines.

They embrace.

SCENE 15

Curtains are pulled back to reveal Pontius and an angry crowd.
They strike a tableau for a moment.

PILATE. Listen, men of Judea! Behold these two – one with gentle countenance, the other a convicted robber and murderer –

CROWD. Free Barabas!

PILATE. I appeal to your human sympathy. Here is Jesus of Nazareth – of worthy bearing –

CROWD. Crucify him! Crucify him!

PILATE. No! I cannot condemn this Man, for I find in Him no guilt. I cannot, I dare not, condemn the innocent!

CROWD. Crucify him! Crucify him! Death to the false Messiah!

PILATE. Bring me water! You compel me by your violence. Take Him away and crucify Him! But know! I wash my hands of it. I am innocent of this blood.

Pilate washes his hands.

CROWD. We take it upon ourselves. His blood be upon us and our children!

PILATE. Therefore I, Pontius Pilate, pronounce this sentence of death on Jesus of Nazareth. But I have no share in this blood-guilt. It falls upon you, and your children. Now, take Him and crucify Him!

Enter the German Officer, dressed in uniform, along with Hitler.

GERMAN OFFICER. If you please, terminate the Passion temporarily in order to welcome our guest and honored friend.

Time stops.
A spotlight on Hitler.

HITLER. *(to the audience, a private moment)* Do you know who I am? You will think, perhaps, years later, that you know me from black and white colors. But black and white are not colors, although they are useful things. I have a strong desire to tell you about the colors – I was once a painter, you see – how one of my eyes has flecks of gold swimming in the brown…the people, they fell in love with my voice, but the women, they fell in love with my eyes – The dark protects us. Our eyes are the same color in the dark. Well.

I do so love public speaking.

Let me tell you about this village. The old man who played Christ was in his sick bed; a new Christ has stepped forward.

He looks at Eric, with approval.

The old must make way for the young, see. Plants and animals know this – people, stupid and crass – they cling to the vine.

I have come to a chorus of glad cheers. The people are always very glad to see me.

EVERYONE. *(but for the Village Idiot and the Visiting Englishman, who abstain)* Heil!

He turns towards them. They fall silent.
He works himself up into a public rage.
The following text is a quotation from Hitler's remarks.

One of our most important tasks will be to save future generations and to remain forever watchful in the knowledge of the menace of the Jews. For this reason alone it is vital that the Passion Play be continued at Oberammergau; for never has the menace of the Jews been so convincingly portrayed as in this presentation of what happened in the times of the Romans. There one sees in Pontius Pilate a Roman racially and intellectually superior, there he stands out like a firm, clean rock in the middle of the whole muck and mire of the Jews.

Now, continue with your holy play. How I *love* the theater.

The Visiting Englishman snaps a picture.

A bulb flashes.
On with the play.
Eric on the cross.
Heavenly choir music from Part One.
Eric looks up, sanctified. He has a glow upon his face.
Mary 1 and Mary 2 lament at the foot of the cross.
Hitler watches.
The sound of a train whistle and a train speeding across
tracks.

SCENE 16

THE VISITING ENGLISHMAN.

Dearest Harriet,

I am writing to you by train. Forgive me if my penmanship suffers. The Passion was glorious. The young man who played the Christ glowed with some invisible spirit. I daresay it almost made me a convert. Don't worry, dearest, *almost* is the operative word. I am Anglican to my bones.

They had an odd little visitor to the play. Herr Hitler. Made me quite jumpy. Reminded me that I much prefer to stay out of politics and seek shelter in the sanctuary of art.

I long to see you, dear – you and the English countryside at the height of summer, when the light appears to last forever – and one can read out of doors until eleven o'clock! Why hunger for more than that?

SCENE 17

The Foot Soldier and Eric in the forest.

FOOT SOLDIER. I got my orders to leave.

ERIC. So soon?

The Foot Soldier nods.

ERIC. Where are you going, exactly? Do they tell you?

FOOT SOLDIER. To Austria, to Poland, to Belgium, to France, to Russia. *(pause)*
Good-bye, little Christ.

They kiss.

ERIC. And one for Belgium.

Eric kisses him on the neck.

And this one for Poland.

He kisses him on the ear.

This for Austria.

He kisses him on the hand.

And this for France.

He kisses him on the mouth once more.

FOOT SOLDIER. That was most definitely France.

ERIC. And for Russia.

He kisses him on the forehead.

Come back safely.

The sounds of war.

SCENE 19

Violet sits in the forest. She is older now. The sky is red.
She holds her white ribbon.

VIOLET. My white ribbon looks red in the dark. I will scatter my breadcrumbs and so find my way home.

A bird enters.
It is Carpenter 1, dressed in his angel wings from Part One.

Hello! Are you a talking bird or a silent bird?

The bird is silent.

Will you fly me out of the forest, bird?
Poor bird. Your body is too big to fly.

The bird blinks.

Maybe you're hungry. I have a few breadcrumbs. Do you want them? You do. All right then. Peck the crumbs out of my hand. I'll remember my way home. I have to sleep now, bird. Will you watch over me while I sleep? Thank you.

She goes to sleep. The bird puppet leaves.
Eric enters wearing a Nazi uniform. He sits beside her
for a moment. She wakes up.

Oh – you startled me. You've got a new costume.

ERIC. Yes.

VIOLET. It's ugly.

ERIC. I have to take you with me.

VIOLET. Where?

ERIC. I don't know.

VIOLET. Do you remember when you were in the play? How you let me out of a box?

ERIC. That was a long time ago.

VIOLET. Well, you're a man now. Why are they taking me away?

ERIC. You're not a native Oberammergauer.

VIOLET. I lived in the village my whole life.

ERIC. It's different.

VIOLET. Different how?

ERIC. You have different blood.

VIOLET. Jesus was a Jew.

ERIC. Kind of. But not really.

VIOLET. Do you remember your lines from the play? Many shall come in my name saying "I am Christ" and shall deceive the multitudes. For false Christs and false prophets shall rise. The sun shall be darkened and the moon shall not give her light. Take heed. Watch and pray; lest coming suddenly He find you sleeping.

ERIC. You have a good memory.

VIOLET. Yes. I do.

ERIC. I'm sorry. We need to go.

VIOLET. Let's play a game. It's called would you rather. Would you rather kill a dog or kick a baby?

ERIC. How hard would I have to kick the baby?

VIOLET. So hard that her head was dented.

ERIC. Kill a dog, I guess.

VIOLET. Would you rather be deaf or poke someone in the eardrum with a needle so that they became deaf? It's a hard one, isn't it?

Eric nods.

ERIC. Poke someone in the eardrum, I suppose. It would be terrible to be deaf. I love music. Come on, now. We don't have time for games.

VIOLET. Please, before you take me, tell me just one story. Tell me the story of Little Red Riding Hood.

ERIC. Well, there was a little girl, wasn't there? She went to visit her grandmother, and her grandmother was a wolf. The wolf ate the little girl.

VIOLET. Yes – that's right. The Englishman didn't know the ending.

ERIC. Will you come with me now?

VIOLET. I always liked you. You don't have a jolly fat face like the other villagers – you always looked a little bit sad.

If the struggle against evil could be contained in one commonplace phrase, "thank you" is the only one allowed to Eric for the moment.

ERIC. Thank you.

A pause.
He extends his hand to take her away.

VIOLET. Wait. Right now – it's not like being in a play – no one's watching – you could do something different.

ERIC. They watch all the time.

VIOLET. Even so – even if they watch you every second of the day – even if they give you a costume and boots and a hat – even then you're not in a play! You're a man. And a man must decide for himself what he wants to do!

ERIC. Look – I can't talk to you. They're waiting. Let's go. Now, take my hand.

VIOLET. No!

A physical struggle between them.
He picks her up.

ERIC. I'll have to carry you then.

VIOLET. Please don't.
      I'd rather walk.

He puts her down.
They are still, facing out.

EPILOGUE

The rest of the cast enters the stage.
They look at Violet and Eric.
They look at the audience.
The sound of a train speeding across tracks.
Eric gives Violet a final push forward into the light.
The lights change from red to grey.
A terrible silence.

Intermission.

PASSION PLAY

PART THREE

Spearfish, South Dakota, 1969 – the present

CHARACTERS

P . . . . plays Pontius Pilate and Satan
(was Pontius the Fish Gutter in Part One)

J . . . . plays Jesus; P's brother
(was John the Fisherman in Part One)

MARY 1 . . . . plays the Virgin Mary
(was Mary 1 in Part One)

MARY 2 . . . . plays Mary Magdalen
(was Mary 2 in Part One)

VA PSYCHIATRIST . . . . also plays ensemble roles
(was Visiting Friar in Part One)

VIOLET . . . . .Mary 1's child,
three years old when we first meet her
(was Village Idiot in Part One)

CARPENTER 1   . . . . also plays ensemble roles and bird
(was Carpenter 1 in Part One)

CARPENTER 2   . . . . also plays ensemble roles
(was Carpenter 2 in Part One)

DIRECTOR . . . . (was Director in Parts One and Two)

YOUNG DIRECTOR . . . . (was Machinist in Part One)

RONALD REAGAN . . . . also plays Queen Elizabeth and Hitler

NOTES ON CASTING

There is some flexibility in terms of how to cast the ensemble roles;
one of the Carpenters or the Visiting Englishman could play the Young
Director, for example. The special effects guy could be played by the
Machinist (which makes sense thematically); but if one of the Carpenters
or the Visiting Englishman is more suited to the role, so be it. However,
it seems important that the Visiting Friar become the VA Psychiatrist in
terms of the transition toward secular confession in the modern world...

SET

Open space.
The suggestion of a tollbooth.
A horizon line.

1970: Spiritual need as there never was before. The turning away from
God and modern man's flight before the world to come have in this
world led to perplexity, helplessness, and resignation, to a fight of all
against all... Man wanting to be like God and to redeem himself by
his own strength has failed deplorably. Is this the reason why scores of
people flock to Oberammergau?"

– Dr. Karl Ipser,
Das Passions Spiel Obermmergau,
official illustrated catalogue, 1970

ACT ONE

ONE: PROLOGUE

ENSEMBLE.
Spearfish, South Dakota, 1969!
Picture red earth
dead tribes
knickknacks, ghost towns –
big signs for miles
telling you, something's comin' –
the corn palace –
a real palace made entirely out of corn,
that's right, corn –
Ever been to the badlands?
You could go crazy
one stretch of rock looks
just like another stretch of rock.
In French the badlands means something like
this land is not so good for living in
but not many people speak French out here anymore.
Keep going, keep driving –
You'll pass the Battle of Wounded Knee
wasn't really a battle, more like a massacre –
it snowed a lot that day – the blood got covered up.
Drive past the Harley convention,
people riding with their beards
flapping in the wind.
Keep going, keep driving –
you're smack dab in the middle of this country –
the Black Hills all around –
then you'll hit exit twelve:
the Passion Play of South Dakota.

TWO: 1969 – BACKSTAGE

Backstage at the Passion Play
after a performance.
J, who plays Jesus,
and P, who plays Pontius Pilate.
They're brothers.
They're taking off their costumes
and their makeup and drinking cold sodas.
It's hot out.

J. People were crying today, front row. I was glad, for your last one.

P. Till I come back.

J. That's what I meant.

Mom wants everyone up at the house tonight. Everyone's real proud.

P. Yeah. You'll look after Mary when I'm gone, won't you?

J. Course I will.

P. I wanted to give you something before I left.

He gets out a reel to reel.

J. Music?

P. No, I recorded the wind. On top of the mountain.

J. You're always doing something funny.

P. I thought maybe you could use it, for concentration – help you study.

J. Uh – thanks.

P. So, what are they teaching you – up there at the university?

J. Philosophy.

P. Who you at now?

J. Saint Augustine.

P. Aw, Saint Augustine. Good stuff. Gotten to the part where he goes to the hooker?

J. I'm behind.

P. Well, he goes to a hooker.

J. But he's a saint.

P. I know. But he repents. That's the whole thing – he repents.

J. I bet they have hookers overseas.

P. I'll be thinking about Mary.

J. I know. Just kidding.

Look – thanks for the wind thing.

I mean it. I'll miss you.

P. Don't talk like that.

A Crowd enters, all dressed in Biblical costume.
The wind stops.

CROWD. Surprise!

For he's a jolly good fellow, for he's a jolly good fellow, for he's a jolly good fellow, which nobody can deny!

P. You didn't have to do this!

Mary 1 enters in her Virgin Mary costume.
She carries in a cake with candles.

MARY 1. Make a wish.

P. It's not my birthday.

MARY 1. But your birthday'll be over there. We're celebrating early.

P. Okay.

He blows the candles out.
P and Mary 1 kiss.

P. Wanna know what I wished for?

MARY 1. It's against the rules!

P. Okay, I won't tell you. I'll show you.

He gets down on his knees.

P. Will you?

MARY 1. Did you plan this?

P. Got the ring right here!

He takes the ring out of his Pontius uniform.
Queen Elizabeth enters, slow, silent.
Everyone suspends,
P kneeling before Mary 1.

QUEEN ELIZABETH. My loving people.
I am resolved to live or die amongst you all, to lay down, for my God, and for my kingdom, my honor and my blood. For I am married to England!

She takes P's ring for a moment.
She considers the ring. She puts it on her wedding finger.

We shall shortly have a famous victory over the enemies of my God!

Queen Elizabeth places her hand on P's head as he kneels.

Go forth into battle, my son! And go with God!

She places the ring on Mary 1's finger.
She moves to exit.
Mary 2 snaps a polaroid, a flash.
The scene continues as before.

P. *(to Mary 1)* Take that veil off!

She does.
He kisses her.
Everyone finishes singing:
"For he's a jolly good fellow, which nobody can deny!"
Queen Elizabeth slowly processes across the stage, waving to the crowd.
She exits.
No one notices.

THREE

A backstage tour, out of time.

MARY 2. *(to the audience)* That was the day everyone remembered. The day Pontius Pilate proposed to the Virgin Mary. Here's a polaroid I snapped – see, Pontius Pilate is kneeling down...proposing to my sister back stage.

I play Mary Magdalen. I'm not much of an actor. I do the play because I believe in the message. It's a message of love. Questions?

Questions from the backstage tour ensemble:

ENSEMBLE 1. Have you acted anywhere else?

MARY 2. Nah. I don't like the city. I like being in a place where you can see the horizon. I like to see what's coming at me. Even if it's bad.

ENSEMBLE 2. Who's that? *(pointing at an imaginary photograph)*

MARY 2. That's a picture of my father. He started the Passion Play in America – he didn't like how things were going over in Germany. He auditioned over one hundred women for the part of Mary Magdalen. He hired my mother. She was a vaudeville actress from Chicago. They got married and my father – uh – upgraded her to the Virgin Mary.

ENSEMBLE 3. Did they play Christ and the Virgin Mary the whole time they were married?

MARY 2. Sure did.

ENSEMBLE 3. Was that weird?

MARY 2. No, it wasn't weird. It was just how it was.

ENSEMBLE 4. Do you have a day job?

MARY 2. When I'm not in the play I work at the tollbooth out on highway sixteen. The night shift. It's not the most glamorous job in the world. But there's not a lot of jobs out here, not right now.

ENSEMBLE 4. Isn't that dangerous?

MARY 2. Oh, nah...I like to think of myself as a beacon of
     light on a dark night. Funny, huh? Sometimes I press
     a quarter into a stranger's hand in the middle of the
     night and think it's kind of like communion. Who
     knows if they get it. They just drive off, into the night.

FOUR

Mary 1 and P.
Mary 1 wears a bathrobe.
P is dressed in uniform.

P. When your alarm clock goes off in the morning, imagine it's me telling you I love you. Beep beep beep I love you.

MARY 1. Okay. I brought you this to keep in your pocket.

P. The Virgin Mary.

MARY 1. Yeah.

P. So I can keep you in my pocket.

MARY 1. Yeah, me and her.

P. Bye.

He picks up an army bag.
He kisses her.

MARY 1. Bye.

He leaves.
She waves.

Five

Mary 1 and Mary 2, in bathrobes,
helping each other put on makeup for the show.
Mary 1 is dressing as Eve.

MARY 2. Hold still. You got a smudge.

MARY 1. Thanks.

MARY 2. He's gonna be fine.

MARY 1. I know.

MARY 2. So buck up. You gotta put yourself in God's hands.

MARY 1. I hate to sleep alone. My feet get cold. I put socks on and then my feet get hot so I take them off under the blankets but then my feet get cold again in the night. It's unnatural, cold and unnatural, this solitary sleeping.

MARY 2. Maybe you should get a cat. When I'm cold I just put a cat on my feet.

MARY 1. I'm allergic, remember?

MARY 2. Oh, yeah. I think allergies are so weird, don't you? Some people are allergic to their own skin. Why would God create allergies?

MARY 1. Maybe God didn't create allergies. Maybe they just happened.

Mary 2 shrugs.
She makes a final touch to Mary 1's makeup.

MARY 2. God created everything. Even bad things. Right? You're ready to go on, babe.

Mary 1 walks onstage.
An ensemble member playing Satan, dangling an apple,
approaches her.

ENSEMBLE. Eve. Eve.

MARY 1. Who is there?

ENSEMBLE. I – a friend – and for thy good is the coming. Bite on boldly, be not abashed.

MARY 1. I'm sorry – it's just. It's not the same as my husband does it.

SIX

Mary alone, in her bathrobe.
The sound of wind.
She is afraid.
J enters.
She jumps.

MARY 1. Thanks for coming. I got scared. The wind's so loud. Banging around – sounds like other things. I saw a snake today out back.

J. What kind?

MARY 1. I don't know.

J. Did it have a triangle head or a square head?

MARY 1. Didn't get that close to it.

J. I'm sure it was harmless.

MARY 1. Didn't look harmless.

J. You want me to just sit here while you sleep?

MARY 1. Okay. Only I can't sleep.

I made some hot chocolate. Want some?

J. Sure.

She goes to get it.

MARY 1. *(shouting from off)* How's school?

J. Pretty good.

I'm taking some acting classes, actually.

MARY 1. *(from off)* They have acting classes? At the university?

J. Yeah.

MARY 1. *(from off)* Why would you study acting out of books?

J. We get on our feet too. Today we imagined we were smelling lemons. It was amazing.

Mary 1 enters with the hot chocolate.

J. I actually smelled a lemon and there was no lemon there to smell.

MARY 1. Huh.

Well, I don't see why you'd study acting at a college. You already know how to act.

J. Kind of. What we do is community theater, Mary. We all have other jobs.

MARY 1. You want to have acting be your *job* ?

J. Yeah.

MARY 1. Where? New York?

J. Or Los Angeles.

MARY 1. On television?

J. Sure. What?

MARY 1. I just don't picture you on television. That's all.

J. Why not?

MARY 1. Because I know you. You're not supposed to know people on television.

J. Someone has to know them.

MARY 1. I guess.

J. You want some fancy cigarettes?

Might help you sleep better.

MARY 1. I don't smoke that stuff.

J. You mind if I have a little?

MARY 1. No. You smoke that a lot?

J. Not very often. Just in the afternoon, mostly.

MARY 1. Hope you don't do it before the play.

J. I think Jesus would appreciate really good marijuana.

MARY 1. Oh, God.

J. He was a peaceful man.

MARY 1. Shut up.

He takes out a joint and begins smoking it.

J. Any letters?

MARY 1. Just got the first one.

J. What's he say?

MARY 1. Nothing about boot camp. Only those crazy made-up stories he likes to tell.

J. Read it.

MARY 1. I don't know if he'd want me to –

J. I'm his brother!

MARY 1. Well. Okay.

She takes out a letter from her bathrobe pocket.

MARY 1. Dear – Oh, I – I'll skip over that part.

Um –

Once upon a time there was an iron who fell in love
with a wrinkle.

It was a tragedy. The end.

Once upon a time there was a lightbulb

who fell in love with the darkness.

It was a tragedy. The end.

J. He's crazy, my brother.

MARY 1. Don't say that.

J. In a good way.

J exhales.

MARY 1. Smells interesting.

J. Sure you don't want some? You're all wound up. You'll
be up all night.

MARY 1. Maybe I'll try one little bit. Can't hurt.

Don't tell your brother.

J. I won't.

She takes a drag, smoking it like a cigarette.

J. Here – like this. That's how they do it in Woodstock.

He shows her how to smoke it like a joint.

MARY 1. How would you know?

J. I've seen pictures.

MARY 1. Oh.

So.

J. So.

MARY 1. Today, after I did my snake scene, I saw a snake. In
the backyard! Isn't that weird?

J. Yeah, that's the reason I came over, remember?

MARY 1. Oh, yeah. I forgot. *(She laughs.)*

The weird thing is that while I was looking at it, it was pretty, not scary at all. It was only *after* I saw it I was scared. What's scary about a snake is not the Bible stuff – I think it's that a snake doesn't have legs and arms and still it can kill you. I'm not afraid of bears because you can *wrestle* with a bear, you understand how it thinks, how it wants to hit you cause it's angry. But how can you understand something with no arms and no legs that wants to kill you – no wrestling, no holding each other – just one bite and it's gone. Your whole life.

J. You're stoned.

MARY 1. No, I'm not.

Must be the hot chocolate.

J. Right. Don't you have that wind tape? Supposed to help you sleep?

MARY 1. I don't like the wind. It makes me afraid.

J. What are you afraid of, d'you think?

MARY 1. The wind makes me feel lonely.

J. I think I'm stoned.

MARY 1. Oh.

J. You're stoned, too.

MARY 1. I'm not stoned, I'm loney.

J. You're not loney, you're stoned.

MARY 1. I'm not loney, I'm stones.

J. That's right, you're stones, loney.

They kiss.

MARY 1. Wait. Who are you?

J. I'm just the guy who came over to stop the wind.

They kiss some more.
The sound of a gunshot.

SEVEN

*P, in his uniform, drags a huge, bloody fish across the
stage.
He holds a smoking gun.
A smear of blood across the stage. A red sky. Elizabethan
fish puppet music.
A bright light –*

P. My head!

> *P collapses.
> Queen Elizabeth enters.*

QUEEN ELIZABETH. I cannot fathom why any subject would
be willing to *die* for any leader other than a *monarch.*
What man would *die* for a leader who was not *rushing*
to the battle-field with him – their blood soaking into
the dust together. On the battle-field the monarch and
the nation's blood are one! *(She touches P.)* Are you
wounded, soldier?

P. I – I killed a fish.

QUEEN ELIZABETH. May God keep you.
Carry him off the battle-field!
Now!

> *Big beautiful fish puppets enter.
> The Carpenters, dressed as Elizabethan courtiers, carry
> P offstage.
> The Queen examines the smoking gun, curious.
> She carries it offstage.*

EIGHT

Mary 2 in her tollbooth, alone.
Night. Rain. Cars on the other side of the highway
pass by, their headlights across her face.
She sings a song to herself.
She sings to the tune of "Away in a Manger."

MARY 2. *(making it up as she goes along)* Away in a tollbooth
No room for his bed
No cars for an hour
To rest his sweet head –
I look for an angel –
I look for a – car
But no one comes by me
For hour upon hour.

Mary 2 looks out the window.
Mary 1 appears. Mary 2 is startled.

What are you doing here this time of night?

MARY 1. You busy?

MARY 2. Naw. No cars for an hour. You're soaking wet.

MARY 1. I had to talk to you.

MARY 2. Shoot.

MARY 1. If you thought you were – and you didn't want to be – what would you do? Would you get a – ? What would you do?

MARY 2. But you're married. So it doesn't matter if you're –

MARY 1. I know, but just say I didn't want –

MARY 2. Mary, that's –

MARY 1. What?

MARY 2. A sin. Are you – ?

MARY 1. I don't know.

MARY 2. Breasts? Vomit?

MARY 1. Yes.

MARY 2. Well, you're married. So –

MARY 1. I know.

But if I – would you forgive me – if I – ?

Mary 2 nods.

MARY 2. You're my sister.

MARY 1. And you won't tell?

MARY 2. That I forgave you for something I don't know about?

MARY 1. Yeah.

MARY 2. No – I won't tell. But have you – already?

MARY 1. No. Thought maybe I'd get some kinda sign.

MARY 2. Mary.

The beams from a car approach.

MARY 1. *(Thinking that it's a sign from the natural world)* Oh my God –

MARY 2. Car coming. Duck down.

Mary 1 kneels down, making the tollbooth look almost like a confessional.
A car approaches.
We see neither the car nor the passenger, only light.

Here's your change, sir. Have a good night.

The car drives off.

I hate when they don't say good night.
No one's got any manners these days.

NINE

J and Mary 1 at rehearsal, the next day.
J on the cross.
Mary 1 kneeling down by it.

J. *(as Jesus)* Eloi, Eloi, lama sabachthani!

MARY 1. *(as the Virgin Mary)* Why, why is my son slain!

DIRECTOR. There needs to be more – um – anguish from both of you.

J. I just – I don't know if I can do this moment out of context. Without the arc of the whole play, you know, to get me there.

DIRECTOR. The arc of the play.

J. Yeah. I'm serious. You have to go through the whole play to get there.

DIRECTOR. We can't run the whole show right now.

J. I know.

DIRECTOR. Then what are you suggesting?

J. It's just that – I've known these lines forever – and it feels stale – and I'm sorry, but I don't feel like you're giving me any direction.

DIRECTOR. Is this what happens when you go to college? You turn into a prick.

J. I just want the play to be good.

DIRECTOR. Well. Me too.

J. So how do you want me to play this moment.

DIRECTOR. *(turning to Mary 1)* Can you speak his language?

MARY 1. *(to J)* You want it to feel real, right?

J. Yeah.

MARY 1. Well, have you ever been betrayed?

J. No.

MARY 1. That's too bad. Do you know anyone who's been betrayed?

J. Yes.

MARY 1. Then why don't you use that.

DIRECTOR. Okay. That's fine. Use it. Let's go.

J. Eloi, Eloi, lama sabachthani! No. It wasn't right. I wasn't feeling it.

DIRECTOR. It was better.

MARY 1. No! It wasn't better! You're still *acting*! My father – he never acted – he just told the story. There was no – effort. There was no – acting.

DIRECTOR. It's not really appropriate for one actor to give another actor notes. If any direction needs to be given, I will give it. Now, let's try that again.

J. I don't want to rehearse this moment, okay? I'll get it right, in performance, when it happens.

DIRECTOR. Fine. Let's move on. Mary, let's have your line.

MARY 1. *(no emotion)* Why? Why is my son slain?

DIRECTOR. Why don't you try rocking back and forth on that line. Hold your arms to your chest.

MARY 1. *(with no emotion, rocking back and forth)* Why? Why is my son slain?

DIRECTOR. *(to Mary 1)* What's wrong with you?

MARY 1. He's not even saying his lines!

DIRECTOR. If we can't get along in a *theater* when the world is falling apart then how can you expect anyone to get along in this world? There's a war on. Why don't you do it again. And think about *that*.

MARY 1. I don't want to think about –

DIRECTOR. Now take a deep breath –

MARY 1. But it's –

DIRECTOR. Then go.

J and Mary 1 take a breath.

J. Eloi, Eloi, lama sabachthani!

MARY 1. Why, why is my son slain?

DIRECTOR. Again.

J. Eloi, Eloi, lama sabachthani!

MARY 1. Why, why is my son slain?

Mary 1 weeps.

DIRECTOR. Again.

J. Eloi, Eloi, lama sabachthani!

MARY 1. Why, why is my son slain?

DIRECTOR. Okay.

> *(to J)* You can get down from the cross now.

J gets off the cross.

> *(to Mary 1)* Can you repeat that in front of an audience?

J. Yeah.

Mary nods.

DIRECTOR. Good. It's going to be a long day. Take five minutes. I have to talk to the lighting designer. We have to tech the ascension.

The Director exits.

J. Look, I'm sorry, okay. That never happened.

MARY 1. What never happened?

J. You know what.

MARY 1. Don't talk to me.

J. Mary, I've been in love with you since the seventh grade or longer and I'll never say another word about it.

MARY 1. What?

The Director and ensemble enter.

DIRECTOR. Lights up! Get on the platform!

J gets on the ascension platform.

Everyone in the tableau!

The ensemble makes the ascension tableau.

Can we hear the music?

Music swells. A reprise of the heavenly choir music from Part One.

DIRECTOR. Now, slowly move your arms up towards Jesus!
    In time to the music! (*to the crew*) More light! No we
    want it *back*-lit! On the scrim! More smoke! (*to J*) Are
    you rigged? Are you strapped in? Now lift him up.

J flies up.

Now the clouds part. The clouds part! Now look up
at Him! Smile up at Jesus! That's right! Now everyone
freeze! And – black-out.

Blackout.

ACT TWO

ONE: PILATE COMES HOME

P hesitates outside a door.
Mary 1 enters.

MARY 1. You ready to come in?

P. Almost. Can't believe it's you.

Let me just –

He traces her cheek.

Is it you?

MARY 1. It's me, honey.

She traces his cheek.
He winces.

P. Oh –

MARY 1. What did I – ?

P. Don't touch me yet, okay.

MARY 1. Okay. Why don't you touch me?

He touches her hands.

P. *(to the audience)* She is a deer wrapped in brown velvet.

She is the air breathing inside the body of a violin.

MARY 1. What?

P. Nothing.

Sorry.

I'm not being myself, am I?

You know that funny phrase – what is it – remember me to your mother. I need you to remember me – to myself. Can you – ?

MARY 1. Think so.

Here we go – I'm remembering you to yourself.

She touches his forehead.
He winces.
Violet enters.

VIOLET. Daddy!

P. Violet! The pictures of you were pretty. But not half so pretty as you.

VIOLET. I drew you a picture of a bird.

P. Wow! How is it you can draw such a good bird, only three years old?

VIOLET. I'm good at drawing birds.

P. That's the best bird I ever saw. It's so good I bet it even flies.

He flies the bird picture around the room.
He picks up Violet and flies her around the room.

VIOLET. *(laughing)* Put me down!

P flies crazier.

Put me down! I'm scared!

MARY 1. You're scaring her, honey.

P puts her down.

P. I didn't scare you, honey, did I? We're just playing bird.

VIOLET. I know.

MARY 1. Why don't we all go to sleep. It's been a long day.

P. I'll sleep right here, just outside the door. You two call me if you need anything.

MARY 1. What? Why, honey?

P. So I can hear.

MARY 1. Hear what?

P. If anyone's coming.

MARY 1. No one's coming.

P. Not right now. But when we're *sleeping*. When you sleep outside you can hear the leaves if anyone's coming. I want to protect you. And Violet.

MARY 1. I know, honey. But it's safe here. It's South Dakota. Remember?

VIOLET. Why is Daddy sleeping outside?

P. To protect you from bad people.

VIOLET. Are there bad people tonight?

P. There are always bad people.

Mary 1 gives P a blanket.

Goodnight.

Sleep with the angels, Violet.

VIOLET. What's that mean?

P. Sweet dreams.

Mary 1 and Violet exit.
P curls up in his blanket.
He looks at the sky.
The sky is red.
He sits up.

(to the audience) Red sky at night, sailor's delight.
Red sky at morning, sailors take warning.

The chorus enters with wind machines
and Elizabethan boats.

They're coming through the fog to the shore, the tall
ships, and I'm making sure they get here safe...real
safe...I feel a gale of wind coming from the north but
I counter it with a gale from the south...I pour wind
into their sails, and it's important they get here by
morning...

P steers the boats through the wind, conducting.
Violet enters.

You should be sleeping.

VIOLET. You should be sleeping.

Why are there boats in the sky?

P. You can see them?

VIOLET. Yes

P. It's a secret, but your dad can control the wind.

VIOLET. Really?

P. Yep. See, when I was in the war I was the pilot of a ship.

VIOLET. And you blew the wind yourself?

P. That's right. So I could push my ship exactly where I needed to go. That way I never made a mistake.

VIOLET. When I was in the war, I was not a pilot.

The chorus exits.

P. What do you mean, honey? What war?

VIOLET. The war before.

P. Before what?

VIOLET. There is always a war before, and a war after.

P. Before this war you were safe, safe in your mother's stomach.

VIOLET. Nope. There was a war before. I died.

P. You shouldn't be thinking about wars. You're only a little girl. Get those wars out of your head.

VIOLET. You get the wars out of *your* head.

P. How?

*She tries to pluck the war
out of his head with her fingers.
She puts it on the ground.*

Now you.

He does the same to her.

There they are, two wars side-by-side.

They look at the wars.

Are they gone?

VIOLET. No.

Almost.

Jump on them.

They hold hands. They jump.

TWO

J and P.
In the dressing room,
getting ready for rehearsal, putting on costumes.

J. You look good.

P. You look good too.

   You need a hair-cut.

J. It's for the play.

P. Oh, yeah.

   What ever happened to wigs?

J. I wanted it to look real.

P. Well, it looks like – real hair.

   So.

   I hear you been acting all over the place – summer stock yards?

J. Summer stock.

P. Good parts?

J. Pretty good. People think it's kind of funny, me playing Christ. They get a kick out of it, actually.

P. So it's – kind of like a gimmick?

J. I didn't say that.

P. Well what is it then?

J. It's just a – nothing. Look – there have been some changes in the play, since you've been gone. Mary write to you about it?

P. She wrote me about other things.

J. Well, there's a new director. A young guy. And it's more professional. There are more professional actors. And there's a real stage manager – not Hank from the garage. And there's a new sound system. It sounds pretty good, actually.

P. Actually. Since when do you say actually all the time – it makes it sound like you think everyone else is a moron. Sorry.

J. It's okay. Really, it's okay.

P. Wonder if I still know my lines.

J. My kingdom is not of this world.

P. Thou art a king then.

J. You still got it.

THREE – A Rehearsal

P and J in costume.
Mary 1 and Mary 2 in costume.
Violet, dressed as a shepherdess.
The whole ensemble.
Including a brand-new director,
and a special effects expert.

YOUNG DIRECTOR. *(to P)* At this point, when you do the Satan bit, we're adding firecrackers. So you sort of shoot firecrackers out of your arms, like this.

SPECIAL EFFECTS. They're regulation firecrackers. Completely safe. You just pull the cord, and whammo.

He shoots firecrackers out of his arms.
P winces at the firecrackers.

P. Sorry, I can't do firecrackers today.

YOUNG DIRECTOR. Okay, we'll work the firecrackers tomorrow. Let's move on to the second act. From: "I cannot condemn him."

P. *(as Pontius)* I cannot condemn him. What has this man done? Look at his face, so gentle in countenance.

ENSEMBLE. Crucify him! Crucify him!

P. I will do as you say. But look – I wash my hands!

P washes his hands. He sees blood everywhere.

Oh, there's so much blood…

YOUNG DIRECTOR. Hold on.

What's the matter?

P. Is this fake blood or real blood?

YOUNG DIRECTOR. It's water.

J. You okay?

P. It looks like blood.

YOUNG DIRECTOR. Maybe the water's rusty. Can we go on?

P. I, Pontius Pilate, at the desire of the whole Jewish people – condemn this man to death. Now, take him and crucify him.

Hitler appears.

P sees him.
No one else does.

HITLER. Do you know who I am?

P. *(to Hitler)* You'd better get out of here.

YOUNG DIRECTOR. Excuse me?

Hitler stands there, between P and the Young Director.

P. Sorry. What was I doing – washing the blood?

YOUNG DIRECTOR. That's right. Let's just take it from your line: I, Pontius Pilate –

P. I, Pontius Pilate, at the desire of the whole Jewish people, condemn – Wait. The Jews are saying: kill Jesus! But they're religious men, right? And Pilate was a bad guy, a tyrant. How come they want to kill him and I'm being all heroic – like – no, no, I can't kill him?

YOUNG DIRECTOR. The Jews want to kill Jesus because He's too powerful.

That's how it's written in the Bible.

Isn't it?

MARY 2. Kind of.

MARY 1. We're just telling the story, honey, the story from the Bible.

P. Just telling the story, bullshit! Either the Jews killed Jesus or else they're innocent!

YOUNG DIRECTOR. Look, we've had the Anti-Defamation League here, haven't we?

CARPENTER 2. *(to the Young Director)* Oh, yeah they came, about six years ago, and gave us some feed-back. Used to be we had horns on the costumes of the high priests but we took them off a long time ago – um – six years ago. So the Anti-Defamation League – now they really – um – like our play.

P. I don't care about a fucking league, I'm talking about a man, a real man.

YOUNG DIRECTOR. I think we need to get away from talking about the play as a real historical document and get back to the play as a *play*. It is our task as actors to –

MARY 2. It's not just a play! It's the word of God!

DIRECTOR. Yes, of course. Can we move on now?

P. Move on, move on, who cares about anything as long as we move on…

DIRECTOR.	**P.**
Look, I know you've had a rough time of it, but we only have one day until dress rehearsal –	I don't want your pity, I want to know what's going on in this fucking scene! *(to HITLER) GO AWAY!*

Hitler walks offstage.

YOUNG DIRECTOR. Are you all right?

P. Yeah, yeah, I'm all right.

YOUNG DIRECTOR. Let's just take it from there – from: I, Pontius Pilate –

P. Okay. But I want to change it. I'm gonna say: I, Pontius Pilate, an agent of the State, condemn this man to death. Not the Jews, not history. *I* will take responsibility. Now take him and crucify him.

MARY 2. That's not what the Bible says.

P. The Bible says lots of things.

YOUNG DIRECTOR. Do you want to go outside?

P. I don't want to hit you.

YOUNG DIRECTOR. Then don't hit me.

A silent moment between P and the Young Director.

YOUNG DIRECTOR. Let's take it from your line.

P. I, Pontius Pilate, an agent of the State, condemn this man to death. *I will take responsibility.* Now take him and crucify him.

ENSEMBLE. Oh, happy day for the people of Israel! Long live our Governor, Pontius Pilate!

YOUNG DIRECTOR. Thank you. Now exit stage left.

P looks left and right, forgetting what stage left means.

Double time, soldier.

P passes by the Young Director.
P clocks the Young Director.
A brief tableau.

FOUR

Mary 1 and the Young Director, who has an ice pack on his cheek.

YOUNG DIRECTOR. I'm going to have to fire your husband.

MARY 1. Look – give him another chance.

He just got home. He's not himself.

YOUNG DIRECTOR. I'm trying to put on a *professional* production –

MARY 1. – of the Gospel. You know how it'd look – in this town – if you fired a soldier?

YOUNG DIRECTOR. How?

MARY 1. Bad. 'Specially you just back from Canada.

YOUNG DIRECTOR. I'll give him one more chance. One.

MARY 1. His understudy's out in Oklahoma anyway.

YOUNG DIRECTOR. He's not in Oklahoma. He's in "*Oklahoma!*"

MARY 1. What?

YOUNG DIRECTOR. Forget it.

FIVE

The sky is red.
P, alone, up high,
assembling jars full of wind.
He stacks them.

P. Red sky, at night, sailor's delight.

He takes a jar, traps some air, screws the lid on.
Mary 1 appears.

MARY 1. What are you doing all the way up here?

P. I wanted some air.

He traps some more air in a jar.

MARY 1. You mean – as in – to breathe it?

P. Yeah. And to keep it. Here –
the night air. Perfect, like you.

MARY 1. Thanks, honey.

P. Look how red the sky is.

MARY 1. It's probably just the – nuclear reactor – next town
over.

P. Maybe.
Or something bigger.

They look at the horizon, holding hands.

So, there was some stuff that wasn't in my letters.

MARY 1. You don't have to tell me.

P. I want to.
I was powering a ship that had a gunner on the back.
And there were lots of explosions – all the time – felt
like they were right here *(pointing to his head)*. But one
time, we heard a huge explosion, and we heard people
screaming, so we went ashore to help out. I was holding a little girl – maybe Violet's age. Her head was in
my hands, and it was wet, and I realized her whole skull
was – gone – and her brains, in my hands – on my
clothes – and for a long time we thought the enemy
shot into the camp, because we thought who would kill

women and children like that – but later I realized no – we were shooting into the woodline. It was us.

MARY 1. It's not your fault.

P. There were no showers, you know – we were in country on February 28th – I didn't shower until May 10th. I washed my hands without water:

He rubs his hands together.

Ponitus Pilate – with no water.

MARY 1. Honey.

P. And I would think of old Pilate, lying there in the dark. How Pilate had good intentions – he *had* to kill someone innocent, it was all part of the big plan. He saved us all, didn't he, by being willing to be bad. But – a little girl's brains – there's no plan for that.

MARY 1. You're a good man.

P. Yeah, right. I don't want to be in the play anymore.

MARY 1. What? Why not?

P. I don't believe in God anymore.

MARY 1. It's okay – a lot of people don't believe in God these days –

P. No – it's not okay! In this town – people *should* believe in God – or else they're fucking hypocrites! You believe in God, don't you Mary –

MARY. Yes, I believe in God –

P. Tell me you're the same, you're the same –

MARY 1. I'm the same honey, I'm the same –

He kisses her.

P. I still have the Virgin Mary in my pocket, see?

He shows her.

SIX

A rehearsal
The whole company.
Carpenters working on the cross.
Violet is dressed as a shepherdess.
The acting style is broad, gestural.

P. *(as Pontius)* Art thou the King of the Jews!

J. *(as Jesus)* Thou sayest so.

P. Hearest thou not how many accusations they hurl at thee? Why art thou silent?

J. My kingdom is not –
Wait, can we stop?

YOUNG DIRECTOR. Okay.

J. I was thinking about this scene. And I thought it would be better if we toned it down. Just – real. Two men talking.

YOUNG DIRECTOR. In an amphitheater for six thousand people.

J. Could you mike us?

YOUNG DIRECTOR. We can hardly see your faces. Look – we need the physical *gesture*.

J. Well, I don't want to do it this way, this grand gesture stuff. It's fake. I want to do it for real.

P. For real.

J. Yeah, for real.

P. What do you mean real?
It's not real.

J. I want people to feel the *humanity* of it.

P. Are you saying how I'm acting isn't human enough?

J. I'm not saying anything about your acting.

P. Sure you are. You're saying I'm not real enough

J. I –

P. You don't need to pussy foot around me, for fuck's sake, just say you don't like the way I'm doing the scene.

A moment of danger.

J. Yeah, I don't like the way you're doing the scene. Actually.

P. What the fuck do you know about real? You want real?

J. Yeah.

P. You want real?

J. Yeah.

P finds a nail on stage, and a hammer, by the cross.

P. This nail is real.

J. Stop it.

P. This wood is real.

MARY 1. Calm down honey.

P. And my hand is real.

    You want to know about real sacrifice?

    It's in the body.

P puts his left hand on the cross, palm up.
He holds a nail with his left fingers and points it towards
his palm.
With his right hand,
he hammers the nail into the palm of his hand.
The world goes into slow motion.
The women scream.
Mary 1 turns Violet's head away.
P doesn't scream.

Blackout.

SEVEN: 1984

A clinical feeling.
P and a VA psychiatrist at a VA hospital.
P's left hand is limp, crushed, at his side.

VA. What year is it?

P. October.

VA. What *year* is it?

P. Oh.

VA. It's 1984.

Who's president?

P. The actor.

VA. President Reagan, good, that's right.

I see in your records that you had a suicide attempt in 1974, that you were hospitalized for a month in a South Dakota VA.

P. It wasn't a suicide attempt.

VA. No?

P. No. I crucified Pontius Pilate. I figured why not crucify the bad guy for once, you know?

VA. You're the bad guy?

P. No, I played the *role* of a bad guy. It's a metaphor.

VA. It says in your records that you were given medicines for delusions. Are you still on medication?

P. Ran out.

VA. I spoke to your wife on the phone today.

P. Ex.

VA. Okay. Ex. When's the last time you talked to your ex-wife?

P. Probably talked to her today. This morning.

VA. She said she hasn't talked to you in a year.

P. She doesn't talk to me but I talk to her.

VA. She mentioned that you think you can control the wind?

P. Did she?

VA. How do you know that you can control the wind?

P. The Lord told me so.

> *P smiles.*

> Just kidding.

VA. Do you think you can talk to God?

P. I talk to him but he doesn't talk to me.

VA. Well, that's a common enough problem.

P. I guess.

VA. Your wife also said you wanted to kill the President.

P. No. He's a good President. He gave me a raise. Three hundred dollars. Spent it on cigarettes.

VA. It says in your records that you've been in ten different cities at ten different VAs over the past ten years. You seem to travel a lot. Why'd you leave home?

P. I like to sleep outside. Look – I didn't come here to confess my sins to you. Unless you can absolve me of my sins, and I don't think you're qualified to do that, and I don't see any holy water in your office, just give me a pill, a pill for my troubles, a pill please. I have a really big king-sized headache. I thought about shooting myself to make my headache go away but I thought you might have like a really really big asprin.

VA. I'll see what I can do.

> *He looks down at his chart.*

P. Is this all we've got now? A bunch of white coats? No priests to say yes, son, your suffering meant something, no kings on the battlefield to say, yes, soldier, your suffering meant something. Just give me a pill, a God-shaped pill please.

> *The VA Psychiatrist looks up from his chart.*

VA. I'm trying to help you.

P. Yeah, thanks. Sorry. Look – I just want to get myself back to South Dakota.

VA. And what'll you do when you get there?

P. I'll play Pontius Pilate the way he was meant to be played.

VA. And how's that?

P. Like a hung-over politician in a God-forsaken province
who took stupid orders on a really fucking bad day.

EIGHT

P pressed up against Mary 1, kissing her.

P. *(almost incomprehensible)* Kiss me harder, into my heart…

He kisses her.

MARY. I'm your ex-wife, goddamit, wake up –

P.	**MARY 1.**
I just need somewhere to sleep, honey.	You've been drinking –
I just need a shower –	

MARY 1. My God! You can't just *pop in* every couple of years and take a shower here! How do you think that is for Violet? You could go to the church –

P. I don't need a church. I need soap. And a razor.

MARY 1. What for?

P. Pontius Pilate didn't have a beard.

He was a Roman. He was clean-shaven.

MARY 1.	**P.**
There's no rehearsal honey –	I'm going to talk to the director –
there's no Pontius Pilate –	get my part back –
Someone else has it now!	
A professional actor.	
From Nebraska.	

P. Oh, really a professional?

MARY 1.	**P.**
That's right.	From *Nebraska?*

MARY 1. He went to school – he's Equity – I don't know.

P. Is he better than me?

MARY 1. He's fine.

Yeah, he's good.

P. Really. Can he show what it's like to give orders to kill a man? Unless he's been there and seen what it's like up close –

MARY 1. *(overlapping with his "up close")*
Yeah, yeah, up close –
I've heard this before –
You can't stay here.
Where the hell have you been?

P.
I killed people – for that man – and no one wants to give me a fucking bar of soap!

MARY 1. What man?

P. The President, who else.

MARY 1. There's another President in the White House now, honey.

P. Take your pick! A likeable man becomes a tyrant just like any other man. In a democracy – likeability is tantamount to tyranny

MARY 1. Tantamount?

P. Tantamount.

MARY 1. You're drunk.

P. No – I'm not drunk! In a democracy, it is a *likeable* man who gets elected. It is a *likeable* man who sends you to your death. What's the difference.

MARY 1. There's a difference between a – a – likeable man and an evil man.

P. I can tell you, you don't *feel* the difference, when everyone gets zipped up in a body bag, and no one says anything about it, they just say "ZIP!" Because when there are guts where skin should be – and skin, where guts should be – there's no difference between a nice guy and an evil guy who sent you out to kill. One of them is *photogenic* – the other one isn't – they both take you and they go ZIP.

MARY 1. I'm sorry for the bad things that have happened to you.

P. I don't want your pity.

MARY 1. Then what do you want?

P. A shower.

MARY 1. One night.

P. I won't touch you, honey!

MARY 1. *(leaving the room)* Don't call me honey!

P. And could I please borrow a toothbrush?

> *She leaves the room.*
> *She throws a pillow and blanket into the room.*
> *She throws a toothbrush into the room.*
> *She throws toothpaste into the room.*
> *She shuts her door.*
> *Violet enters.*

Violet!

VIOLET. I crawled out the back to see you.

Did you get my bird pictures in the mail?

P. Yeah. You're getting real good with the bird pictures.

VIOLET. I've been learning about the architecture of feathers. The way they're put together – layer upon layer. From the time of dinosaurs and angels. There is no homologue for feathers, that is to say there is no biological structure that resembles feathers. They came of themselves to the world because the birds needed them. But no one knows what came first, the bird, or the feather, or flight.

P. What grade are you in now?

VIOLET. Sixth.

P. There must be a God.

VIOLET. Why'd you come back?

P. I want my part back.

VIOLET. Someone else has it now.

P. I heard.

VIOLET. Then why'd you come back.

P. To see you.

VIOLET. Then why'd you leave?

P. I had to.

VIOLET. Oh.

    Can I see your hand?
    P gives her his hand.
    She drops it up and down, limp.
    She kisses his dead hand.

P. Thanks.

    J enters.

    What are you doing here?

J. What are you doing here?

P. I'm on a visit.

J. I'm on a visit, too.

P. Kind of late in the evening for a visit.

J. Yeah, Violet, you should be in bed.

VIOLET. Don't tell me what to do.

P. Thought you were in New York, L.A., something like that.

J. I was.

P. So what are you doing here.

J. They wanted me back for a benefit performance of the play. The President's here, campaigning. He's going to watch it.

P. Really. You're doing the play for the President of the United States. Pretty fancy. It's my lucky day. I've been meaning to talk to the President.

    Don't they put you up at a hotel?

J. Yeah. But I'm sick of hotels. Thought I'd see if the couch was available.

P. I reserved the couch.

    Mary went to bed.

    You want me to wake her up so you can say hello?

J. No.

    I'm gonna head back to the hotel.

P. No. Stick around. Tell me about your life.

    You married? Have kids?

J. No.

P. Why not? Famous actor, good-looking…

J. Look, where the hell have you been, you could have called, told someone where the hell you landed.

P. No one wants to read letters from me.

I'm crazy, didn't they tell you?

J. I didn't need an expert to tell me that, actually.

P. Oh. By the way, I don't care that you've been fucking my wife, *actually.* You should know that.

J. Violet, go inside.

VIOLET. No.

J. Don't talk like that in front of her.

P. You heard me.

Ignore the curse word, Violet.

I'm making a larger and more important point:

love's more important than fucking. That'll be important for your teenage years.

(to J) Do you agree that love is more important than fucking?

J. Yes, it is.

P. So you admit it then!

J. You want to talk about love? You selfish piece of shit. You want to talk about love? I've been supporting this family for the last ten years.

(P moves towards J.)

P. Yes, I want to talk about love. I'm dying to. Brotherly love. Christ's love for his disciples! Mary's love for her child! And the most glorious – the most profound love of all – the actor's great love of himself! You vain puffed up little turd! Come here!

P grabs J. A scuffle.

(over the scuffle) Am I my brother's keeper? Am I my brother's keeper?

J. No, you're not!

VIOLET. Stop it! Stop it!

They suspend.

Did you know that orca whales are the only species who kill each other for fun, besides human beings? Did you know that, Dad?

P.   **J.**

No.   No.

P. What?

MARY 1. Who's out there?

P. It's only the wind.

(to J) Good night.

VIOLET. *(to J)* Good night.

J. *(to both)* Good night.

Nine: The Play

The tail end of "The Star Spangled Banner," sung by the ensemble.
Ronald Reagan with a hand over his heart, in a spotlight.
The song ends. Reagan waves his cowboy hat, and settles the crowd.
He gives a public speech.

REAGAN. Why, hello everyone. It's morning in America. Isn't it? I believe it is. The dawning of a…new dawn. But, make no mistake, Armageddon is coming. With metal horses and tanks and a red sky. I intend to stop it. God has a plan for me. I was once a lifeguard on the Rock River you know. Saved seventy-seven lives. If the tide is too much for you, I will save you.

I was at Mr. Gorbachev's over there in Moscow. His son's goldfish died. I replaced it. You think history is made by great wheels set in motion. Well it is. But it's also made by small acts of generosity. I replaced a little boy's goldfish and a wall came crumbling down. Mr. Gorbachev, tear down that wall!

Bob Hope once said what's it like being President and I said, it's like being an actor. Only you get to make up the lines yourself. Well that's not really true. Mr. Gorbachev, tear down that wall! How's that sound?

My fellow Americans, we are a God-fearing nation. And God loves this country. Yes, He does. But we are in need of a great spiritual revival.

Cheering.
A light from the camera. A close up shot.
A private speech.

I always liked the light from the camera. The light would go on and I would relax. All I saw was the light.

People say I wear a little rouge on my cheeks. It's not true. When I am laid to rest my cheeks will be rosy still. My campaign manager said what can we do to get those ratings up. Get shot again I said. It was a joke.

REAGAN. *(cont.)* You know what my first job was? A radio announcer for baseball games in Chicago. And you know what? I never even saw the ball games. The games were in Chicago, I was in Davenport, Iowa! They would telegraph the plays to me, and I would make the folks feel like they were there, even though I was – elsewhere! That's what a great leader does. You don't even need to be at the game!

Cheering. A public speech.

Yes, this country is need of a great spiritual revival. A brighter future for – everyone. Now people have said I'm not concerned about the poor, about the homeless. Not true. They're homeless, you might say, by choice.

(He winks.)

Now you're about to see a play about those values our country holds dear: family, God, baseball. No, not baseball. God. And family. And in-tact families like Jesus, Mary and Joseph. And God, the Father. Two fathers, I know, but not really two fathers like that, not in that way, no, because those two fathers have the plague and will bring Armageddon down on the pure wheatfields of this land.

He smiles.

It's morning in America. We *are* that city shining on a hill. We are a people chosen by God to settle a promised land. You are that promise. We are that promise. And now, I give you, the greatest story ever told.

Reagan waves and takes his seat. The play begins.
It is now more of a musical. Very professional.
The sing a song.

SONG.

I will go

To the Father

And sit at His right side.

I will go
To the Father
The world to glorify.

MARY 1. My son! I must see you before you go away.

J. Mother, I am on my way to Jerusalem. The hour has
come when I must offer myself.

MARY 1. Oh, my fears are terrible –

J. My hour has come.

MARY 1. I will go with you, even to death!

Mary 1 is acting better than she ever has in her life.

J. Be comforted. I will rise again.

MARY 1. Ah, God, give me strength that my heart does not
break!

Reagan watches.
He wipes tears from his eyes.
Mary 1 and J embrace, full of love.
It is an odd extended moment.
They look into each other's eyes,
less like the Virgin Mary and Jesus and more like lovers.
P, from the audience.

P. Mary!

The scene suspends. Time stops.

(To the audience) Ever get the feeling
that you want to run on stage?
You want to move,
but you can't?
It's this horrible feeling,
as though you will run on stage
and speak lines all garbled –
lines you made up yourself?

REAGAN. *(To the audience)* I began to think of baseball.
Making it feel real for the crowds.
On the radio.
Bottom of the ninth.

The wind is *gusting* at Wrigley Field.
And now, the wind up. And the
pitch –

P. This big stage
this stage of history,
this little block of wood
separates you from your most terrible fantasies –
it's important, this piece of wood, this stage, between
you and it –

REAGAN. Batter swings – and it's a long fly ball to left field
– and now my telegraph goes dead – it's dead – and I
have to make it all up myself – it's long fly ball, ladies
and gentlemen, and it's going, and it's going – and its
gone!

The crowd goes wild.

P. MARY!
Stop the play!

Everyone onstage finally hears him. People are frozen.

Well, hello Mr. President.

Reagan salutes P.
P salutes Reagan.

REAGAN. I never did serve in the military, but I feel as
though I did. I made training films for soldiers during
the war. It was one of the happiest times in my life.

Reagan salutes P.
P salutes Reagan.

What's the matter son? Don'tcha have a part in the
play?

P. No, Mr. President, I don't.
Mary, I love you.
I always did.

P pulls out a gun.
A secret service agent leaps for P.
P points the gun at himself.
Blackout.

TEN: EPILOGUE – THE PRESENT

Lights up on P,
whose hand is limp at his side.

P. You might think, at the very end, that I'd kill my brother. Kill myself. Kill my ex-wife. Big love triangle, bang bang, an American Passion Play. But that's not how the story ends. I sat in my seat, and whispered: Mary, stop the play, and an old woman next to me said: shh.

I left the theater that day. Every month I take a bus to a different city. I sleep outside. That way I can hear the wind.

I send part of my disability check to Mary every month. She gives backstage tours at the theater. They replaced her with a professional actor. Sometimes I watch my brother on television. He's on a soap opera. I can read what happens to his character in line at the grocery store. They have these – little magazines.

I have a P.O. box. Violet sends me pictures of birds. Every year since she was a kid they looked more and more like real birds. Then she went to college, became a painter, and since then, every year, they started looking less and less like real birds. She looks like my brother but she's crazy like me, so who knows.

I started to believe in God again lately. Something about the light at night on a Greyhound bus going by a tollbooth. I think God is a tollbooth worker. Only he doesn't give exact change. You hand him a dollar, he gives you a fish. Go figure.

I don't know if this country needs more religion or less of it. Seems to me everyone needs a good night's sleep. That way we'd all wake up for real in the morning. It's good to be awake. When you're awake you can fight for what you believe in, no matter what costume you're wearing. Well. The more I talk the less you sleep.

I'll summon the wind for you, so you can sleep better. (The good people at the VA hospital got rid of most of my delusions but I like to keep one or two around.)

Now: wind.

(He conducts the wind.) From the south. To the west.
There.

Good night. Sweet dreams.

Sleep with the angels, Violet.

The wind machines.

The boats. The courtiers.

Big, beautiful fish puppets.

The sky turns white.

P gets on an enormous boat.

He opens his left hand to the sky.

He sails off into the distance.

The End

ACKNOWLEDGMENTS

When you have been working on a play for the past fourteen years, as I have on *Passion Play*, there are many people to thank. But the biggest debt of thanks is due to Paula Vogel, who encouraged me to write my first full-length play, which became the first act of *Passion Play*. She and I would sit at a little café in Providence on Wickenden Street called Café Zog and she would buy me a cookie and read ten pages of *Passion Play*. Had Paula not said: "I think you should write that play," with the characteristic gleam in her eye, I would now be dissecting the imagery of wax in the Victorian novel. I would never have had the strange audacity to write the first sentence of a full-length play. At that time I wrote primarily poetry and fiction, and Paula snuck *Passion Play* into the New Plays festival at Trinity Repertory Company. Seeing that production, directed beautifully by Peter DuBois, was what made me decide to become a playwright. I arrived at the production after a car accident on Hope street where I blacked out, woke up, showed up to Trinity Rep down the hill, saw *Passion Play*, and then the next fourteen years unfolded. Thank you, dear Paula.

Three children and seven plays later, I finally finished *Passion Play* to get it ready for a production in Brooklyn at a beautiful old church, produced by Epic Theater. Along the way, here are the people who helped to birth this play: Molly Smith, who beautifully directed the first incarnation of all three plays and commissioned the third act along with Wendy Goldberg who was then at Arena Stage; Mark Bly who served as dramaturg there; Rebecca Brown who did many readings of *Passion Play* in New York. And these wonderful actors who helped greatly with the process at Sundance, Arena Stage, Brown University, and Lincoln Center Theater: Jefferson Mays, Felix Solis, Howard Overshown, Amelia Campbell, Annabel Capper, Michael Cerveris, Alan Cox, Carson Elrod, David Greenspan, Marin Ireland, Polly Noonan, Keith Reddin, Thomas Jay Ryan, Daniel Talbott, Joaquin Torres, Rebecca Melsky, and I know I am forgetting to write some of you down who have been in and out of this play over the last fourteen years, I am so sorry and thank you! Thanks to the directors Howard Shalwitz, Shira Piven, Chris Fields, and Scott Illingworth. Thanks also to Tanya Palmer for her dramaturgy.

I am so grateful to the brilliant Mark Wing-Davey, who had the patience and enthusiasm to direct four very different productions, from a production in London that cost 200 pounds, to one in Chicago that cost quite a bit more, to one at Yale where I think we finished the play, to the site specific one at Epic. Dear Mark, thank you, and someday we will take *Spring Song* on the road. To Peter DuBois who was the very first director I ever collaborated with, and to Oskar Eustis for being the first producer of *Passion Play* and John Emigh for being the first to put on Acts 1 and 2 together. To Bruce Ostler, as ever. To Bob Falls for having the courage to do a second production of a difficult and large play, and to James Bundy for understanding that sometimes playwrights need a third production to finish their rewrites. And thanks to Zak Berkman for having the vision and patience to put on *Passion Play* in an old church in Brooklyn.

Thank you to my parents who always entertained my metaphysical doubts even while they sent me to Catholic Sunday school, and to my whole family for helping me to keep the home fires burning while I have been at rehearsals. Finally, thanks to Professor David Hirsch at Brown University who taught me Holocaust Literature, knew Melville inside and out, and who said to me once about a paper: "I am surprised. I would have thought you would have written something larger." Dear Professor Hirsch, I hope this is large enough (at any rate it is long enough), wherever you are now presiding, somewhere in the ether entreating people or shades to be ethical, to be literate, and to be large.

OTHER TITLES AVAILABLE FROM SAMUEL FRENCH

THE CLEAN HOUSE

Sarah Ruhl

Comedy / 1m, 4f / Interior, with inserts

This extraordinary new play by an exciting new voice in the American drama was runner-up for the Pulitzer Prize. After its acclaimed run at Yale Repertory Theatre it was done to equal acclaim at several major theatres coast to coast before winding up off Broadway at Lincoln Center, where it had an extended run. The play takes place in what the author describes as "metaphysical Connecticut", mostly in the home of a married couple who are both doctors. They have hired a housekeeper named Matilde, an aspiring comedian from Brazil who's more interested in coming up with the perfect joke than in housecleaning. Lane, the lady of the house, has an eccentric sister named Virginia who's just nuts about house-cleaning. She and Matilde become fast friends, and Virginia takes over the cleaning while Matilde works on her jokes. Trouble comes when Lane's husband Charles reveals that he has found his soul mate, or "bashert" in a cancer patient named Anna, on whom he has operated. The actors who play Charles and Anna also play Matilde's parents in a series of dream-like memories, as we learn the story about how they literally killed each other with laughter, giving new meaning to the phrase, "I almost died laughing". This theatrical and wildly funny play is a whimsical and poignant look at class, comedy and the true nature of love.

"Fresh, funny...a memorable play, imbued with a melancholy but somehow comforting philosophy: that the messes and disappointments of life are as much a part of its beauty as romantic love and chocolate ice cream, and a perfect punch line can be as sublime as the most wrenchingly lovely aria."
– *The New York Times*

"A rich work about big themes from a young playwright with an original and audacious voice."
– *Variety*

"Casts a spell that had me hooked."
– *The New York Daily News*

OTHER TITLES AVAILABLE FROM SAMUEL FRENCH

EURYDICE

Sarah Ruhl

Dramatic Comedy / 5m, 2f / Unit Set

In *Eurydice,* Sarah Ruhl reimagines the classic myth of Orpheus through the eyes of its heroine. Dying too young on her wedding day, Eurydice must journey to the underworld, where she reunites with her father and struggles to remember her lost love. With contemporary characters, ingenious plot twists, and breathtaking visual effects, the play is a fresh look at a timeless love story.

OTHER TITLES AVAILABLE FROM SAMUEL FRENCH

IN THE NEXT ROOM OR THE VIBRATOR PLAY

Sarah Ruhl

Dramatic Comedy / 3m, 4f / Interior

In the Next Room or the vibrator play is a comedy about marriage, intimacy, and electricity. Set in the 1880s at the dawn of the age of electricity and based on the bizarre historical fact that doctors used vibrators to treat 'hysterical' women (and some men), the play centers on a doctor and his wife and how his new therapy affects their entire household.

In a seemingly perfect, well-to-do Victorian home, proper gentleman and scientist Dr. Givings has innocently invented an extraordinary new device for treating "hysteria" in women (and occasionally men): the vibrator. Adjacent to the doctor's laboratory, his young and energetic wife tries to tend to their newborn daughter—and wonders exactly what is going on in the next room. When a new "hysterical" patient and her husband bring a wet nurse and their own complicated relationship into the doctor's home, Dr. and Mrs. Givings must examine the nature of their own marriage, and what it truly means to love someone.

"Insightful, fresh and funny, the play is as rich in thought as it is in feeling…one of the most gifted and adventurous American playwrights to emerge in recent years…*In the Next Room* is a true novelty: a sex comedy designed not for sniggering teenage boys — or grown men who wish they were still sniggering teenage boys — but for adults with open hearts and minds."
– *The New York Times*

"If Henrik Ibsen and Oscar Wilde had decided to collaborate on a post-modern drawing-room comedy, the hotsy-totsy twosome surely would have turned out something very much like Sarah Ruhl's genuinely hysterical new work"
– *TheatreMania.com*

OTHER TITLES AVAILABLE FROM SAMUEL FRENCH

DEAD MAN'S CELL PHONE

Sarah Ruhl

Dramatic Comedy / 2m, 4f / Unit Set

An incessantly ringing cell phone in a quiet café. A stranger at the next table who has had enough. And a dead man—with a lot of loose ends. So begins *Dead Man's Cell Phone*, a wildly imaginative new comedy by MacArthur "Genius" Grant recipient and Pulitzer Prize finalist, Sarah Ruhl, author of *The Clean House* and *Eurydice*. A work about how we memorialize the dead—and how that remembering changes us—it is the odyssey of a woman forced to confront her own assumptions about morality, redemption, and the need to connect in a technologically obsessed world.

"Satire is her oxygen...In her new oddball comedy, *Dead Man's Cell Phone*, Sarah Ruhl is forever vital in her lyrical and biting takes on how we behave."
– *The Washington Post*

"Ruhl's zany probe of the razor-thin line between life and death delivers a fresh and humorous look at the times we live in."
– *Variety*

"[Ruhl] tackles big ideas with a voice that entertains"
– *NPR*

"...beguiling new comedy...Ms. Ruhl's work blends the mundane and the metaphysical, the blunt and the obscure, the patently bizarre and the bizarrely moving."
– *The New York Times*